B. K. Peirce

Audubon's Adventures

Life in the woods

B. K. Peirce

Audubon's Adventures
Life in the woods

ISBN/EAN: 9783337094812

Printed in Europe, USA, Canada, Australia, Japan

Cover: Foto ©Andreas Hilbeck / pixelio.de

More available books at **www.hansebooks.com**

No. 720

Audubon and Family going down the Ohio.

See page 37.

AUDUBON'S ADVENTURES

OR

LIFE IN THE WOODS

BY B. K. PEIRCE, D.D.

EIGHT ILLUSTRATIONS

NEW YORK: HUNT & EATON
CINCINNATI: CRANSTON & STOWE
1889

INTRODUCTION.

THE adventures of John James Audubon will never lose their interest to young or old. His was one of the most unique characters our country has yet given to the world. Great in intellectual endowment, gentle-hearted, and sincerely devout, he was at the same time so thoroughly original, so full of lively incident was his career, and so ivid were his powers of description, that the mere tory of his life is far more interesting than most ovels. The love he bore in his heart for all living creatures was like the love of a brother. He followed them through forest and over plain, on this continent and in Europe, regardless of what risks he ran, if only he might be admitted into the private nooks of Nature and have her secrets revealed to him as to a favorite. Few soldiers have passed through more startling episodes than he; and this little book, if it had no other value than the delightful and varied story it tells, would be worthy of high praise.

But it will be of far greater use than merely to while away an idle hour if the young readers of this volume shall learn from it the value of those habits of close observation which made Audubon the great naturalist of America. Darwin and Wallace have alike borne testimony to the fact that close scrutiny of the animals and plants within easy reach is of greater value than the memorization of volumes. If our young friends will watch the cats and dogs and flies, the rose-bushes and vines

and elms, which are in and around their homes—
watch them with a loving and tireless observation
—they will do more toward their own thorough
education, more toward the acquisition of schol-
arly habits, than the wisest and best of teachers
can accomplish upon them in double the time.
Dr. Darwin in his old age was fond of relating a
practical joke which his little granddaughter
once innocently practiced upon him. She had
sat for two hours watching a favorite cat asleep
on a rug. When her grandfather entered the
room she said, "I have followed your advice,
grandpapa, and have watched the cat, as well as
read about her; and I have discovered that cats
have something which no other quadrupeds possess; what do you think it is?" The old naturalist began at once a mental comparison of cats'
teeth and whiskers and fur and tail and claws
with those of other quadrupeds, but he could not
recall any feline characteristic which was not
shared by other animals. And when he "gave
up" the little girl demurely answered, "Kittens."
It was an innocent and frolicsome conundrum,
but never seemed silly to the great philosopher.
To him it was of value as an evidence of that
freshness of mind which always accompanies
habits of observation. As we read this grace-
fully-written record of Audubon's delightful adventures let us try to imitate him in his close
and loving study of nature.   R. R. D.

  August 1, 1889.

CONTENTS.

CHAPTER I.
STUDY OF NATURAL HISTORY.

CHAPTER II.
EARLY YEARS OF AUDUBON.

CHAPTER III.

AUDUBON'S UNCONQUERABLE PASSION FOR NATURAL HISTORY.

CHAPTER IV.

LIFE IN KENTUCKY.

CHAPTER V.

AUDUBON'S ADVENTURES.

CHAPTER VI.

AUDUBON'S STUDIES IN NATURAL HISTORY.

CHAPTER VII.

AUDUBON'S EXPERIENCE IN PUBLISHING.

CHAPTER VIII.

FROM FLORIDA TO LABRADOR.

8 CONTENTS.

CHAPTER IX.

AUDUBON'S CLOSING LABORS.

Illustrations.

LIFE IN THE WOODS;

OR,

THE ADVENTURES OF AUDUBON.

———◆◆———

CHAPTER I.

STUDY OF NATURAL HISTORY.

I WISH to tell my young readers the strange and interesting story of Audubon, the great American Naturalist, who passed so many years of his life in the woods with the birds, listening to their songs and learning their habits. I hardly think that I should recommend to any one of them to follow his example fully; but it would add greatly to the enjoyment of every one if, in addition to his other studies and labors, he cultivated a taste for some branch of natural history.

With a very little time and attention any one may become familiar with the name and distinguishing marks of the principal rocks upon the surface of the earth, and collect around him a very large and beautiful cabinet. Some of the most delightful hours of his life will be passed in gathering new specimens for his collection. He will always have an entertaining occupation for his spare moments, and a peculiar source of pleasure in all his journeyings. I have known a busy physician to find sufficient time to collect a cabinet that a college was thankful enough to receive, and the enjoyments of his life were increased manyfold.

I have known others acquire a taste for flowers; not cultivated flowers merely, but the charming wild flowers with which God has made the wayside and the meadow to blossom. I recollect meeting, some years since, a delightful old gentleman wearing the plain and neat Quaker dress. He had acquired a handsome property in business, and was devoting the most of his time to benevolent objects. Wherever he went he carried a little, convenient flower-case with him, and whenever his quick eye fell upon a new blossom, or even an old one if particularly attractive, he gathered it as a great prize, and with marked pleasure added it to the treasures of his case. He seemed to know each flower by name; all about its habits, and almost to be able to hold conversation with it.

I shall not soon forget the great pleasure an eminent physician once exhibited when shown a very large elm-tree. He had his tape measure out of his pocket at once to measure it. It proved to be a giant in circumference, and all the facts about it were carefully noted down in his diary. He was acquainted with nearly every very large tree in the state, and every interesting circumstance connected with them. He was familiar with all the different species of trees, and every grove and forest he passed through afforded him inexpressible delight in their examination.

The reason why we do not feel the same enjoyment in these things is, that we have never become acquainted with all the interesting facts about them; just as when a stranger comes into the place where we live, we feel but very little interest in him at first, but after we are introduced to him and become fully acquainted with him we wish to be in his society as often as possible. It will add more to our enjoyment in life, whatever our business or profession may be, than can be told in words, to have some one branch of science or nature so well understood as to enable us to perceive all its beauties.

A great professor was about to lecture before a class of students, and he placed a grasshopper upon the table before them and told them that this insect would be the subject of his conversation for the hour. The young men laughed aloud at this, not thinking that anything new could be said about this little skipping fellow they had seen so often. But they found the hour was only too short, and that their interest increased every moment as the professor opened before them all the singular habits and the facts that he had discovered by long and careful observation about the grasshopper.

One may live a very busy life, and may not have much money to expend, and still surround himself with many objects of interest and profit. A merchant in Boston, doing a very large business, found time, and no ordinary pleasure in the work besides, to collect in his library copies of nearly all the different editions of the Bible that have been published since the invention of the art of printing ; and another gentleman who began life poor, a leather dresser, who continued in his trade until his death, improved his mind and his taste in reading during all his leisure moments, and by economy secured one of the largest and most valuable private libraries in the country.

But perhaps there is no study that will afford more pleasure, nor one that can be so readily and successfully undertaken as that of the habits of the thousand different varieties of birds that make our groves beautiful with their elegant plumage, and melodious with their charming songs. The study has been made very easy and delightful for us by the long, unwearied, but pleasant labors of such men as John James Audubon. What was to them the work of years to learn, and required their passing many months at a time in untraveled forests, and in portions of the country far from human habitations, we may, in a good degree, acquire by simply studying the delightful pages they have written. We should seek, however, to unite personal observation with our reading, and with a volume in our hands giving an account of the different birds that throughout the year frequent our gardens, and fields, and forests, we should seek to identify each one of them, and be able to call by name every songster of the grove.   We shall see, in the life of Audubon, what exquisite pleasure the study of the birds afforded him; and how their habits exhibited the wisdom, love, and providence of their great Creator.

CHAPTER II.

EARLY YEARS OF AUDUBON.

THE parents of Audubon were French Protestants, who were forced by Catholic persecutions to fly from France, and sought refuge in what is now the State of Louisiana, when it was a Spanish colony. It afterward came into the possession of the French, and was, at a still later period, sold by the Emperor Napoleon to the United States. Audubon's father was, previous to his coming to America, an admiral in the French navy. He had a cultivated mind, and was well prepared to undertake the task that fell to him, of watching over the early training of his son. He seems to have been a devout man, turning the thoughts of his son constantly from the beautiful creatures of God to the great Creator himself. This habit followed the son throughout his career. Alone, amid the wilds of nature, for long spaces of time, he seemed to himself to be immediately in the presence and within the providential arms of his heavenly Father; and every

new discovery he made among the feathered
songsters awakened his mind to a livelier
appreciation of the wisdom and goodness of
God.

John James was born May 4, 1780. His
parents were then living upon a plantation,
away from the more thickly settled portions
of the country. From his first recollections
he had a very strong love for everything in
the beautiful world around him. He did not
enjoy the restraints of the house, but wished
to be out among the flowers and the birds.
His father was his constant companion,
pointing out to him everything worthy of
notice, administering to his peculiar passion
for birds and flowers by obtaining all in his
power far and near. He would point out
the elegant movements, the beauty and softness of plumage, their manner of exhibiting
pleasure or a sense of danger, of the birds,
and the always perfect forms and splendid
attire of the flowers. "My valued precep-
tor," says the dutiful son, speaking of him
when he had become himself advanced in
years, and his father had long been slumbering in the dust, "would then speak of the
departure and return of birds with the seasons, and would describe their haunts and,

more wonderful than all, their change of
livery (plumage) ; thus exciting me to study
them, and to raise my mind toward their
Creator."

Young Audubon's love for nature increased with his years. Not satisfied with feasting his eyes upon the birds, he desired to
possess them, and make them his constant
companions. His father sought to gratify
this wish with his gun, and by carefully pre-
serving the birds that he thus obtained; but
with the death of the bird all Audubon's
pleasure in it ceased. "The moment," he
said, " a bird was dead, however beautiful
it had been when in life, the pleasure arising
from the possession of it became blunted ;
and although the greatest care was bestowed on endeavors to preserve the appearance
of nature, I looked upon its vesture as more
than sullied ; it could no longer be said to
be fresh from the hands of its Maker. I
wished to possess all the productions of
nature, but I wished life with them."

He told his father his disappointment, and
with rare intelligence and kindness he
sought to turn this feeling to the best account. He procured for him a book of
illustrations. A new life, he says, ran

2

through his veins when he first turned over the leaves of his new acquisition. It was not indeed just what he wanted, but it suggested to him what became the great pursuit and pleasure of his after-life. The desire was at once awakened in his mind to copy what he saw in the world around him. His pencil now became his constant companion. His earliest efforts were very unsatisfactory to himself. In the book that his father gave him the illustrations were, in his opinion, far from being true to nature, and many of them decidedly bad; but he was mortified to see that his own efforts were greatly inferior even to these. He was not, however, to be discouraged. He kept himself constantly at the work, although annually, on his birthday, he was accustomed to commit to the flames hundreds of the rude sketches that he had drawn with so much perseverance. It was this earnestness and perseverance in his purposes that made him what he afterward became. As we shall see, he was constantly overcoming difficulties that would have discouraged an ordinary mind "Perseverance conquers all things;" and every day's labor, although unsatisfactory, improved his hand and his eye,

and trained him for the extraordinary success that he afterward attained.

When he had reached his fifteenth year
his father, seeing the decided bent of his
mind, sent him to France to study drawing,
under the tuition of the celebrated painter,
David. He remained there two years, prac-
ticing drawing. This was dry work for our
young lover of nature. He panted for his
birds and his fields. He wanted to draw
from the beautiful world itself, and not to
copy the monotonous works of other men.
His laborious training, however, under David, as uninteresting as it might have been,
was undoubtedly of great service to him.
After two years he returned again to his beloved native land.

His father looked upon these studies in
drawing simply as affording pleasure and
profit for his leisure hours, and intended
that his son should engage in commercial
pursuits. Arrangements were made for his
entering into partnership with a young French
gentleman, and he came north that he might
more successfully carry out his mercantile
plans. His father purchased a fine estate for
him in Pennsylvania, upon the Schuylkill
River: its broad fields and extensive wood-

lands offering, however, powerful tempta-
tions for his pencil, and beguiling him from
the less congenial duties incident to a business life.

The plantation of Audubon sloped to a
creek which bore the name of Perkioming.
The scenery around was peculiarly adapted
to awaken the liveliest pleasure in the heart
of one so fond of nature as Audubon. He
was very fond of rambling along its rocky
banks, watching the wild flowers as they
opened in their season, observing the habits
of the kingfisher, perched on some projecting stone over the clear water of the stream,
following with his eye the path of the fish
hawk, followed by the white-headed eagle,
and permitting all these varying objects to
bear "his thoughts," he says, "far above
them into the heavens, silently leading me
to the admiration of the sublime Creator of
all."

Opening upon the creek was a cave, scooped
out of the rock, of sufficient size for him to
make it his study. A circumstance that occurred here awakened a fresh desire to become familiarly acquainted with the habits
of birds. Immediately over the arched en-
entrance of the cave a pewee flycatcher fast-

ened its nest. When Audubon first observed it it was empty. The spring was now opening —the buds having begun to swell upon the trees—when one morning early, as he entered his rocky retreat, a rustling sound overhead attracted his attention, and on turning he saw two birds fly off: the pewees had arrived! As they appeared somewhat surprised and disturbed by his presence, he quietly withdrew and remained away for the day. Early the next morning he hastened to the cave; but they were up before him. Long before he reached the spot his ears were saluted by their well-known notes, and he soon saw them darting through the air, and giving chase to the insects close over the water. They were full of joy, frequently flying in and out of the cave, alighting on a favorite tree near by, and seeming to be engaged in the most interesting conversation. As Audubon approached the cave the male bird flew violently toward the entrance, snapped his bill sharply and repeatedly, accompanying this action with a tremulous rolling note. Presently he flew into the cave and out again with incredible swiftness. Audubon continued daily to visit the cave; after a time he noticed with pleasure that the

birds were becoming quite accustomed to
him, and before a week had passed he and
the birds were on terms of intimacy. The
pewees now began to work at their old
nest.

Having become very much interested in
them, he determined to spend the greater
part of each day in the cave observing their
proceedings. His presence no longer occa-
sioned them the slightest alarm. They brought
fresh materials to renew the nest, lining it
with a few large and soft feathers. There
was a remarkable twittering in their note,
while both sat on the edge of the nest when
repairing it, which is never heard on other
occasions. "It was the soft, tender expression," Audubon says, "I thought, of the
pleasure they both appeared to anticipate in
the future. Their mutual caresses, simple as
they might have seemed to another, and the
delicate manner used by the male to please
his mate, riveted my eyes on the birds, and
excited sensations which I can never forget."

One day the female spent the greater part
of the time upon her nest, frequently changing her position. Her mate exhibited great uneasiness; he would alight by her sometimes,
sit by her side for a moment, and suddenly

flying out, would return with an insect, which she would take from his bill with much apparent satisfaction. About three o'clock in the afternoon the uneasiness of the female increased, and the male looked quite despondent; when suddenly rising up, and looking under her little feet a moment, the female flew from the nest, followed by her consort, performing the most curious evolutions in the air. When they left Audubon peeped into the nest, and saw a little white transparent egg, which was a more pleasant sight to him, he says, than if he had met with a diamond. In a week there were five more. And now the little female pewee, having arranged her eggs and spread her wings, settled down into her nest to hatch her expected brood. The birds took turns in setting upon the eggs. While one was upon the nest the mate could search for food, or, sitting on some adjoining branch, would fill the air with the loudest notes. They had become so tame that Audubon could reach out his hand and lay it gently upon the sitting bird without disturbing it. At the same time he found another pewee's nest attached to the rafters of his mill, and still another in his cattle-yard. He thought, from the perfect similarity of note, that these must all have belonged to the same last year's family; and he afterward found that the brood raised in the cave returned the next spring and established themselves in various places along the creek.

In thirteen days the young birds appeared. The attention of the parents to them was incessant, constantly bringing insects to their little brood. The old birds had become so used to Audubon that they would fly in and out regardless of his presence. He handled the young frequently. Finally he tied small threads to their legs, but at first they were invariably removed. He renewed them until they became used to them, and then he fastened a light silver thread to the leg of each, so loosely as not to hurt it, and so fastened that they could not remove it. They took wing in sixteen days, and the old birds began to arrange the nest for a new brood. These made their appearance in the beginning of August. By the eighth of October every pewee had left his plantation, and all his little companions had taken their first journey to the South.

At the season of their return to Pennsylvania in the spring, Audubon had the satisfaction of welcoming his birds again. The old birds returned to the same nest, and he found several new pewee nests along the banks of the creek. Having caught several of the birds upon the nest, he had the pleasure of finding two with the silver ring upon the leg.

Audubon's business now called him to France, and detained him for two years. But when he returned, in the month of August, he had the pleasure of finding three young pewees in the nest in the cave. Upon examination he found it was not the same nest. The old one had been torn away, and this was placed a little above it. He noticed also that while the male bird allowed him to approach quite near to him, the female was very shy. Upon making inquiry he learned that the miller's son had killed the old mother bird and four young ones (cruel wretch) to make fish-bait. The male pewee had then brought a second partner to the nest.

As long as the plantation of Mill Grove belonged to him, a pewee's nest continued in his favorite retreat

CHAPTER III.

AUDUBON'S UNCONQUERABLE PASSION FOR NATURAL HISTORY.

At this time Audubon married, and commenced a domestic life, which, although
often interrupted by long absence from home
and its beloved inmates, was always a source
of unalloyed enjoyment to him.

His commercial ventures, the demands of
his large farm, and the calls of his little family, could not wean him from the habits and
longings of his childhood and youth.

Day after day he would leave home immediately after light, to wander through the
forests in pursuit of birds, returning only in
the dew of the evening to rejoice over and
draw his newly-acquired prizes.

As might naturally be supposed, with his
mind so drawn aside from business, his commercial speculations turned out badly. He
says of himself in reference to this and the
following years of his life :

" For a period of nearly twenty years my
life was a succession of vicissitudes. I tried

various branches of commerce, but they all proved unprofitable, doubtless because my whole mind was ever filled with my passion for rambling, and admiring those objects of nature from which alone I received the purest gratification. I had to struggle against the will of all who at that period called themselves my friends. I must here, however, except my wife and children. The remarks of my other friends irritated me beyond endurance; and breaking through all bonds, I gave myself entirely up to my pursuits. Any one unacquainted with the extraordinary desire which I then felt, of seeing and judging for myself, would doubtless have pronounced me callous to every sense of duty, and regardless of every interest. I undertook long and tedious journeys, ransacked the woods, the lakes, the prairies, and the shores of the Atlantic. Years were spent away from my family. Yet in all this time I had no other object in view than simply to enjoy the sight of nature."

It was some time later, as we shall see, that he conceived the noble design of giving to others the benefit of his toils, and of rendering invaluable services to the world.

An acquaintance which he formed in Philadelphia, in 1824, with Charles Lucien Bonaparte, himself an enthusiastic naturalist, and a generous friend and encourager of all engaged in like pursuits, gave the earliest definite direction to these labors, which had been undertaken solely for the personal gratification which the study of the wisdom, power, and goodness of God, as exhibited in the animal world, gave to himself. It certainly was no ambition to secure human applause, or to obtain a pecuniary reward. These two leading objects of life appear to have been utterly foreign to Audubon's nature. He only desired that others might share with him his rich enjoyment of nature; and to do this he sacrificed all his fortune, and subjected himself and his family to many of the inconveniences of poverty.

Soon after his marriage, in the prosecution of his business, he had occasion to visit Kentucky and spend two years in Louisville. He had visited the place previously, been charmed with its wild and beautiful scenery; out above all had been won by the hospitality and urbanity of manners exhibited by the inhabitants of this growing town. He and his young wife had no sooner reached the place than, without letters of introduction, they were at once visited by the principal inhabitants of the town. If his business or his rambles in the forests kept him for any length of time from home, his wife was removed to the generous home of some friend in the neighborhood until his return, and when he returned he would be required to extend with her the visit to several weeks. This was true Virginia hospitality, enlarged by all the noble characteristics of the new country into which the citizens of the Old Dominion had emigrated.

His favorite pursuits were by no means forgotten during his residence here. He drew and noted the habits of every bird which he could procure. Every friend who used a gun added to his collection by sending him every specimen that might be of value to him.

While residing in Louisville in 1810 he was visited by Alexander Wilson. Wilson was a Scotch weaver and peddler who had emigrated to this country a number of years before. After working a while at his trade, improving his mind by study and writing, he became the teacher of a seminary in the town

of Kingsessing, on the Schuylkill, a few miles
from Philadelphia.   He here formed the acquaintance of an excellent man, a lover of
natural history, named Bertram, and of an en
graver name Lawson.   From the latter the
studious weaver, who essayed also to be a
poet, took lessons in drawing.

At this time he saw some illustrated volumes of natural history, and a like passion to
that which at an earlier day possessed Audubon, seized upon him. He determined to devote
himself to making a collection of all the finest
birds in the country.   He started out with his
gun, and by engaging the assistance of others,
with the most self-denying labors and persevering efforts to overcome obstacles, he collected the materials, made the drawings, and
published the first volume of his work entitled "American Ornithology."   The second
volume, the materials for which were collected amid difficulties that would have appalled
an ordinary man, was published in January,
1810, and the author started upon a western
and southern tour, both to obtain subscribers
for his work and to add to his collections for
succeeding volumes.

Wilson called upon Audubon to obtain his
name to his list.   "How well do I remem-

ber him," says Audubon, " as he then walked
up to me. His long, rather hooked nose, the
keenness of his eyes, and his prominent cheek
bones, stamped his countenance with a peculiar character. He had two volumes under
his arm, and as he approached the table
where I was working, I thought I discovered
something like astonishment in his countenance. He opened his books, explained the
nature of his occupations, and requested my
patronage. I felt surprised and gratified at
the sight of his volumes, turned over a few
of the plates, and had already taken a pen in
hand to write my name in his favor, when
my partner, rather abruptly, said to me in
French, 'My dear Audubon, what induces
you to subscribe to this work? Your drawings are certainly far better; and again, you
must know as much of the habits of American birds as this gentleman.' Whether Mr.
Wilson understood French or not, or if the
suddenness with which I paused disappointed him, I cannot tell, but I clearly perceived
that he was not pleased."

At Mr. Wilson's request he took down a
large portfolio, and showed him the drawings
that he had made himself. He had now a
collection containing upward of two hund-

red.   Mr. Wilson's surprise was great, as
he had not the most distant idea that any
other individual besides himself was engaged
in such a work. His surprise increased when
Audubon assured him that he had no intention to publish; for as yet the most distant
idea of this had not entered his mind. It is
not impossible that this visit may have
awakened the first thought in this direction.

With the utmost generosity he loaned Mr.
Wilson his drawings during his visit, ex-
plored with him the surrounding woods, and
procured him birds that he had never before
seen. He also offered him any of his drawings, upon the simple condition that his name
should be published in connection with them.
But Wilson had little of Audubon's noble-
ness of soul. He expressed no gratitude, and
made no response to these generous offers;
but when, in a succeeding volume of his work,
he referred to his visit in Louisville, he says,
with absolute untruth and peculiar meanness,
"I neither received one act of civility from
those to whom I was recommended, one subscriber, nor one new bird; though I delivered
my letters, ransacked the woods repeatedly,
and visited all the characters likely to sub

scribe. Science or literature had not one friend in this place."

After two years' residence in Louisville, Audubon returned again for a short period to Pennsylvania.

3

CHAPTER IV.

LIFE IN KENTUCKY.

AUDUBON's business leading him principally to the valleys of the Mississippi and the rivers flowing into it, and this country affording him the richest facilities for gratifying what had now become the absorbing passion of his life, he made his arrangements to leave the vicinity of his first home upon the Schuylkill permanently. His family consisted only of his wife and an infant son. He had fixed upon Henderson, Ky., at that time a small village on the Ohio, about two hundred miles below Louisville.

There were no steamers in those days, or any form of public conveyance, either upon the Ohio or its banks. Taking his infant son and wife, he purchased a large skiff, or *dugout* as it was called, and with a mattress and food, and two negro hands on board as rowers, he started for his new home, floating down the Ohio river.

This beautiful river, now alive from Pittsburgh to its mouth with boats, its banks smil-

ing with numberless cities and villages, rolled
on with no other sound but its own ripples,
or the occasional sharp dashing of an Indian
paddle; and its banks were covered with un-
broken forests, the hunting grounds of sav-
age foes. It was autumn when Audubon
made his voyage, and his mind was deeply
impressed with the wonderful tints which
now decorated the October verdure. "Every
tree," he says, "was hung with long and
flowing festoons of different species of vines,
many loaded with clustered fruits of varied
brilliancy, their rich bronzed carmine min-
gling beautifully with the yellow foliage which
now predominated over the yet green leaves,
reflecting more lively tints from the clear
stream than ever landscape painter portrayed
or poet imagined." Here and there, on the
passage, the lonely cabin of a "squatter," as
the first inhabitants upon the new soil were
called, would strike the eye, giving evidence
of the commencement of civilization. They
met occasionally a flatboat laden with produce from the head of the small rivers flowing into the Ohio, and sometimes with a
company of emigrants, the scouting parties
of the immense armies of pilgrims from other
shores seeking new homes in the unsubdued

but fertile wilds of our western lands. Such
a journey, so long, and marked by so few incidents, would undoubtedly be considered
very wearisome by the most of my readers
in this day when we travel like the wind,
night and day, and are even conscious of an-
noyance often because we do not move even
more rapidly; but Audubon, floating in his
flatboat down the silent Ohio, rarely meeting a human being, says of his feelings, " Pur-
er pleasures I never felt; nor have you,
reader, unless indeed you have felt the like,
and in such company."

After several days of such life as this they
neared their chosen residence. One evening,
approaching what was then called Pigeon
Creek, a small stream running into the Ohio
from the state of Indiana, they heard loud
voices, and imagined that they could distinguish the cry of " murder." They knew that
the Indians in these parts had been uneasy
of late, and had committed many depredations,
making bloody attacks upon the scattered
settlements, and they naturally felt somewhat uncomfortable at the sound of this cry.

When they had floated a little further their
fears were very pleasantly dispelled. It
proved to be a very different cry from " mur-

der" that they heard. They soon came in sight of a Methodist camp-meeting, held under the shade of a beach forest.* It was a cry of life and not of death that they heard. Thus early, when the groves were the only temples, while the Indian tribes were prowling around their scattered dwellings, the itinerant gathered the strange and hardy population for divine worship, and consecrated the rising states in the hour of their helpless infancy to the worship and service of God. Who can estimate the influence of these self-denying pioneers upon the destinies of these immense states, now holding in their hands the balance of power in our country? What would this uneducated people, from different nations, and speaking different tongues, have become had not the faithful minister of Christ immediately followed upon the trail of the emigrant?

After a sail of two hundred miles, they reached their appointed place of landing at Henderson. "When I think of these times," says Audubon, "and call back to my mind the grandeur and beauty of those almost uninhabited shores; when I picture to myself the dense and lofty summits of the forest,

* See Frontispiece.

that everywhere spread along the hills, and
overhung the margins of the stream, unmo-
lested by the ax of the settler; when I
know how dearly purchased the safe naviga-
tion of that river has been by the blood of
many worthy Virginians; when I see that
no longer any aborigines are to be found
there, and the vast herds of elks, deer, and
buffaloes which once pastured on these hills
and in these valleys, making for themselves
great roads to the several salt springs, have
ceased to exist; when I reflect that all this
grand portion of our Union, instead of being
in a state of nature, is now, more or less,
covered with villages, farms, and towns,
where the din of hammers and machinery
is constantly heard; that the woods are fast
disappearing under the ax by day and the
fire by night; that hundreds of steamboats
are gliding to and fro over the whole length
of this majestic river; when I see the surplus
population of Europe coming to assist in the
destruction of the forest, and transplanting
civilization into its darkest recesses; when I
remember these extraordinary changes have
all taken place in the short period of twenty
years, I pause, wonder, and, although I know
all to be fact, can scarcely believe its reality."

Audubon did not yet entirely give up his efforts to better his fortunes by cultivating the openings for trade offered in the new country; but these endeavors being, on the whole, unsuccessful, and the opportunities for pursuing his favorite studies being so numerous and inviting, the largest portion of his time was passed with his gun and pencil in the woods and upon the banks of the mighty rivers of the West. He made wide and frequent excursions, not only into all parts of the neighboring territory, but over a great portion of the inland country of the United States. "Provided with a rough leathern dress, with a knapsack that contained his pencils and his colors, and with a good, trusty gun at his side, he wandered for days, and even months, in search of birds to describe and paint. At one time we find him watching for hours in the tangled cane-brakes of Kentucky, where some shy songster is silently rearing her brood; at another he is scaling the almost inaccessible mountains, where the eagle hovers over its rocky nest; now he is floating in a frail skiff down the rushing tide of the Mississippi, and is carried on he knows not whither by the flood; then the jealous Indian prowls about his lonely path, or lurks beneath the trees on which he sleeps, waiting for an opportunity to put an end to his life and his uncomprehended labors together; here he begs shelter and food in some lonely log-cabin of the frontier, and there he wanders hopelessly through the interminable pine-barrens of Florida, while hunger and thirst, and insects and wild beasts beleaguer his steps like so many persecuting spirits. But wherever he is, whatever lot betides, in difficulty and danger, as well as in the glow of discovery and success, the same high, genial enthusiasm warms him, the same unfaltering purpose sustains and fortifies his soul. The hero on the battle-field never marched to victory more firmly than he marched to the conquests of science and art." *

WONDERFUL ENDURANCE OF A NATIVE HORSE.

While Audubon was residing in Henderson, a gentleman who had just returned from the head-waters of the Arkansas river, where he had purchased a newly-caught "wild horse," a descendant, probably, of

* "Homes of American Authors."

some of the horses originally brought from
Spain, and set at liberty on the Mexican
prairies, having no further use for him,
offered him to Audubon. He was not handsome; he had a large head, and his thick,
uncombed mane hung along his neck to his
breast, and his tail reached nearly to the
ground. His chest was broad, his legs
smooth and sinewy, and his glaring eyes
and wide nostrils indicated spirit and endurance. He had never been shod, and although
he had been ridden hard on a long journey,
his black hoofs had suffered no damage. The
gentleman had traveled upon his back at the
rate of from thirty-five to forty miles a day
without interruption, giving him for food
simply the grass of the prairie and the canes
of the bottom-lands. He wished Audubon
to try him. He found that he moved with
great ease, both to himself and rider. He
leaped a log several feet in diameter back
and forth a number of times with the utmost
ease. To try his strength Audubon drove
him to a swamp muddy and tough. He
entered it with his nose close to the water,
as if to judge its depth, and then dashed
through without flinching. He rode through
the swamp in different directions, and found

him prompt and cheerful. He then drove him to the river, for there are some horses that appear to be unable to swim; they simply lie upon their sides and float with the current; the rider must either swim and drag them to the shore or abandon them. Audubon rode into the Ohio, and the horse made off with his head high out of water, and rather turned against the current, his nostrils expanded and breathing freely. He turned him down the stream, and then again up, but the horse, without discouragement, at once yielded to the bit. When they reached the shore he stopped of his own accord, and spreading his legs, shook the water from himself like a duck, nearly shaking his rider from his seat. After this, putting him upon a gallop, he dashed through the woods, shooting from his saddle a turkey-cock, which the horse immediately approached as it fell, as if he understood what was to be next done, enabling the rider to pick it up without dismounting. Satisfied with the trial, Audubon purchased him for fifty dollars; and business calling him to Philadelphia, he started on Barro, as he called his pony, and taking a circuitous route, rode him two thousand miles, traveling not less than forty miles a day. When he returned his horse was in as good order as when he left. On horseback was at this time almost the only means of traveling, as coaches were very rare, and there were scarcely any roads fit for carriages. Audubon's wife made the journey from Henderson to Philadelphia in the same way. It used to take twenty days to ride from Louisville to Philadelphia, while the journey can now be made in a little more than two.

Barro became so attached to his master, and under such control, that when Audubon reached a clear stream where he desired to bathe, the horse would graze on the bank without fastening, and would not drink if he was told not to do so. On his way homeward from Philadelphia, at the crossing of the Juniata river, a gentleman from New Orleans, named Vincent Nolte, met him. He was mounted upon a superb looking horse, for which he had paid three hundred dollars, and his mounted servant also led another as a change. As Audubon approached he praised the gentleman's horse, who not very courteously remarked that he wished *he* had as good a one. Finding that he was going to Bedford, Audubon asked him at what hour he would reach there.

"Just soon enough," was the answer, "to have some trouts ready for our supper, provided you will join when you get there."

Barro seemed to hear and understand the conversation; he pricked up his ears and lengthened his pace. Mr. Nolte chirruped to his horse, and urged him to a quick trot; but it was all in vain. Audubon reached the hotel a quarter of an hour before him, ordered the trouts, saw that good care was taken of Barro, and stood at the door ready to welcome Mr. Nolte. His acquaintance, made under these amusing circumstances, proved of great service to him. Mr. Nolte became a very warm friend, and when Audubon sailed for Europe gave him the letters to friends in Liverpool by whose encouragement first of all, and more than all others, he was inspired to undertake his great work. It was with regret that his master finally parted with Barro, for nearly three times as much as he cost him.

CHAPTER V.

ADVENTURES OF AUDUBON.

A LIFE in the forests and on the prairies, continued for so many years, could not have passed without adventures. Audubon passed through many strange and some dangerous scenes, but, preserved by a remarkable providence, no serious accident ever befell him.

THE MIDNIGHT ASSASSINS.

Upon his return once from the upper waters of the Mississippi, he was obliged to cross one of the immense open prairies which are the marked features of that portion of our country. His only baggage was his knapsack and his gun, and his dog was his only companion. The brilliancy of the prairie flowers, and the sports of the fawns with their dams, perfectly fearless of the rare spectacle of a man in their haunts, beguiled the hours as he moved slowly on. The sun began to sink beneath the horizon long before he could discover any appearance of woodland, a level ocean of verdure spread out in every direction. He had not met a man during the day. His path was an old Indian track. As night fell upon him he naturally felt a strong desire to reach a grove, where, under some shelter, he might pass the hours of darkness and rest. The distant howling of the wolves gave him some hope that he was approaching a woodland.

His expectations were realized, and as he came to the skirts of the wood his eye was attracted by a fire light, toward which he moved at once, supposing it to proceed from the camp of some wandering Indians.

He was mistaken, however, for it proved to come from the hearth of a small log-cabin, before which a tall figure was passing and repassing, busily engaged in household duties.

The tall figure proved, upon his reaching the place, to be a woman, and Audubon sought shelter of her for the night. With a gruff voice she answered in the affirmative. As he entered and seated himself by the fire, the first object that attracted his attention was a finely formed young Indian, who sat resting his head between his hands, with his elbows upon his knees. A long bow rested against the log wall near him, and a quantity of arrows and two or three raccoon skins lay near to him. He did not move upon Audubon's entrance, and hardly seemed to breathe; but, accustomed as he was to the habits of the Indians, and knowing that they were silent, and paid no attention to the presence of a stranger, he considered this only another illustration of the natural or forced apathy of the red man. Audubon addressed him in French, a language partially known to many of the Indians in this part of the country through their intercourse with the early French fur-traders and Catholic priests. The Indian raised his head, pointed to one of his eyes with his finger, and gave Audubon a significant glance with the other. His face was covered with blood. He learned afterward, that an hour before this, as he was in the act of discharging an arrow at a raccoon, the arrow had split upon the cord, and springing back had destroyed the sight of his eye forever.

Audubon, very hungry from long fasting and his weary walk, began to inquire what fare he might expect. He took a fine timepiece from his pocket, and told the woman that he was much fatigued and wished his supper, that he might go to his rest for the night. The sight of the watch seemed to excite the woman at once. It appeared to strike her fancy wonderfully, and she had to be permitted to enjoy its examination at once. Audubon took off the gold chain that secured it around his neck, and presented it to her for her personal observation. He allowed her to place it upon her own brawny neck, while she expressed her eager desire to be possessed of such a watch. No suspicion of the woman, living as she did in so retired a spot, seems, as yet, to have crossed the mind of Audubon. She told him that there was plenty of venison and jerked (dried) buffalo meat in the house, and that by opening the ashes on the hearth he would find a corn cake. The Indian rose from his seat as if in extreme pain, and passed and repassed him several times. Once he pinched him with so much violence as to call out from him an exclamation of anger. Audubon looked at him, the Indian's eye met his; but his look was so forbidding that it struck a chill to his heart. The Indian again seated himself, drew his butcher knife from its greasy scabbard, examined its edge, and once more replaced it. He then took his toma-

nawk from his back, filled the pipe of it with
tobacco, and continued casting upon him
peculiar glances whenever the woman's
back happened to be turned in the preparation of the supper. The truth began to
dawn upon Audubon's mind, and for the
first moment he began to suspect the danger
that surrounded him; but from the corre-
sponding glances of his silent companion, he
felt confident that in any event the Indian
would be his friend. After supper he asked
the woman for his watch, wound it up, and
under the pretense of desiring to see what
might be the promise of the weather on the
morrow, he took his gun and walked out of
the cabin. He slipped a ball into each barrel, scraped the edges of his flints, renewed
the primings, and returned to the hut, giving
a favorable account of his observations in
reference to the weather. He then took a
few of the bear-skins laying loosely around
the cabin, made a bed in the corner with them,
and calling his faithful dog to his side, he
laid down with his gun close to his body
In a short time he seemed to be soundly
asleep.

Soon voices were heard, and through the
corners of his eyes Audubon saw two stout
4

youths make their entrance, bearing a dead
stag upon a pole between them. Having
disposed of their burden, they asked for
whisky, and helped themselves to it very
freely. Observing the stranger on the bear
skins and the wounded Indian, they asked
their mother (for so she proved to be) who
the lodger was, and why the Indian rascal
was in the house. They knew the Indian
could not understand a word of English.
The mother quieted them, insisting on their
speaking lower, and told them about Audubon's watch. She then took them away into
a corner, and engaged in an animated conversation in a very low tone of voice. He
could readily guess the subject of it. He
tapped his dog gently, and as he wagged
his tail, Audubon noticed that his eyes almost blazed as they were fixed alternately
upon himself and upon the trio whispering
in the corner. The Indian also exchanged
glances with him. The boys drank themselves into such a state as hardly to preserve
their consciousness, and the old woman herself made frequent applications of the whisky
bottle to her mouth. She soon rose, and
taking a large carving-knife, went to the
grindstone to whet its edge. He saw her

deliberately pour on the water, turning the stone with her foot, working away upon the murderous instrument, until the sweat covered his body in spite of his determination and preparation to defend himself. Her task finished, she walked to her reeling sons and said:

"There, that'll soon settle him! and then for the watch."

Audubon turned, cocked his gun-locks silently, and touched his faithful companion. It was a startling moment; all was ready. The fiendish woman advanced slowly, evidently considering the best way of dispatching him, while her sons should be engaged with the Indian. Audubon was several times upon the eve of rising and shooting her upon the spot, but another fate awaited her. The door was suddenly opened, and there entered two stout travelers, each with a rifle on his shoulder. Audubon leaped upon his feet in a moment, and gave them a hearty welcome. The tale of the night was soon told. The drunken sons were properly secured; the woman, in spite of her vigorous self-defense and loud protestations, was also bound. The Indian fairly danced for joy, and gave them to under-

stand, that as he could not sleep for pain, he
would remain on guard during the night.
There was, however, more conversation than
sleep during the night.

When the morning broke the feet of the
prisoners, now well-sobered, were unbound,
their hands being securely tied, and having
set fire to the cabin, as was the custom in
the administration of justice in such cases in
the woods, and bestowed summary punishment in the adjoining grove upon the mur-
derers, they gave the skins and implements
found in the hut to the young Indian, who
was much delighted with the satisfactory
termination of the affair. Perhaps the most
singular fact in connection with this adventure is his assurance, that during his wanderings, extending through a period of more
than twenty-five years, in every portion of
the frontier of our country, this was the
only time when his life was endangered by a
fellow-creature. Not many miles from the
place where this event occurred, then far
from civilized habitations, is now the site of
a thriving town.

THE HEARTY WELCOME IN THE WOODS.

As a fair counterpart to this, showing the true hospitality of the woods to this day, .n a degree characteristic of the dwellers in the log-cabins of the far West, the following night adventure of Audubon may be related.

His son, a stripling, had accompanied him upon an excursion on foot of several hundred miles. As they had become somewhat fatigued, they hired a wagon and driver for the next hundred miles, and jogged on over the rough roads as rapidly as they could. The driver, feeling perfectly familiar with the country, left the main road for a short cut across the country. Before they could reach the road again a terrible storm came upon them, and night, coming earlier on account of the clouds, dark and dismal, settled down upon them. The rain was falling in torrents, and the driver had lost all idea of his direction; the way was rendered dangerous by falling trees, and they could only give loose reins to the horses, and trust to them to draw them out of their forlorn condition. Suddenly the horses altered their course, and soon after they perceived the glimmer of a faint light in the distance. At the same moment they heard the barking of dogs. The horses stopped near a high fence and commenced neighing, while the occupants of the wagon set up a loud shout. The next moment a flaming pine-torch moved through the darkness, and advanced to the spot where they were dripping in their misery. A negro boy bore it, who, without waiting for a question, called upon them to follow the fence, and said that master had sent him to show the strangers to the house.

They soon reached the gate of a little yard, in which a small cabin was discovered. A young man, tall and fine-looking, stood at the open door, and desired them to dismount and come in.

"A bad night this, strangers," said he; "how came you to be near the fence? You must certainly have lost your way, for there is no public road within twenty miles."

"Sure enough," was the answer; "we have lost our way, but, thank God! we have got to a house, and thank *you* for our reception."

"Reception!" replied the woodsman, "no very great thing after all; you are all here safe, and that's enough. Eliza," said he, turning to his wife, "see about some victuals for the strangers; and you, Jupiter," addressing the negro lad, "bring some wood and mend the fire. Eliza, call the boys up, and treat the strangers the best way you can. Come, gentlemen, pull off your wet clothes and draw to the fire. Eliza, bring some socks and a shirt or two."

Mr. Audubon had been so used to the hearty hospitality of the cabin, that he was not so much impressed by this generous reception; but his son, to whom it was all new, whispered to him, "how pleasant it is to meet such good people."

The young wife moved with so much liveliness, that no one could doubt for a moment that her labors for her guests afforded real pleasure to her. The negro boys were busy. The cries of the poultry, startled from their slumbers, gave promise of the coming meal, and the whole cottage was beaming with the rousing fire upon the hearth. The host remarked that it was a pity they had not chanced to come that day three weeks before; "for," said he, "it was our wedding-day, and father gave us a good house-warming. You might have fared better; but if you can eat bacon and eggs and a broiled chicken, you shall have that. I have no whisky in the house, (well that he had not,) but father has some capital cider, and I'll go over and bring a keg of it."

This, as my young temperance readers will see, was long before temperance societies were dreamed of. They asked him how far distant his father lived.

"Only three miles," said he, "and I'll be back before Eliza has cooked your supper."

Sure enough, off he went in his generous zeal, the rain pouring in torrents all the while. The newly married couple were very young. Their means seemed barely sufficient to make them comfortable, but their kindness knew no limit. The cabin was new. The logs, which were of the tulip tree, were nicely stripped of their bark. Every part was clean. The garments of the wife, made of substantial homespun, hung on one side, and those of the husband on the other. A large spinning-wheel, with beautiful rolls of wool and cotton, occupied one corner. In another was a small cupboard, containing the little stock of new dishes, cups, plates, and tin pans. The small table was new, and as bright as polished walnut could be. There was only one bedstead, and this was entirely, together with its bedding, of home manufacture, the counterpane showing the fine skill of the young mistress in weaving. A fine rifle hung over the fireplace. A white cloth soon covered the table, which was at once loaded with the most inviting provisions; and just at this moment the husband's horse was heard clattering without, announcing his return. He bore triumphantly in his keg of cider, saying as he entered,

"Only think, Eliza, father wanted to rob us of the strangers, and was coming here to ask them to his own house, just as if we could not give them enough ourselves. Come, gentlemen," he continued, "draw up to the table and help yourselves."

While they were doing full justice to the meal, the wife resumed her spinning, and the husband waited upon the guests, and to their questions cheerfully gave them an account of his condition and prospects. His father came from Virginia when young, and settled on the large tract of land around them, and by hard work had done well. There were nine children of them, nearly all married and settled in the neighborhood. The old gentleman had divided his land among them. Two years ago he received his portion, and a finer piece could not be found. He had cleared a couple of fields and planted an orchard. His father had given him a small stock of cattle and horses. He had camped most of the time while clearing and planting. When about to marry the young woman then at the wheel, his father had helped him to build his cabin. They had begun life, he thought, as well as most folks, and, the Lord willing, might make themselves a comfortable home. "But, gentlemen," said he, breaking in upon the thread of his story, "you don't eat. Eliza, maybe the strangers would like some milk." The wife at once stopped her work, and hurried to meet the request of her husband.

But now came the arrangements for the night. "Eliza," said the husband, "the gentlemen would like to lie down, I guess. What sort of a bed can you fix for them?" Eliza looked up with a smile and said: . "Why, Willie, we will divide the bedding and arrange half on the floor, on which we can sleep very well; the gentlemen will have the best we can spare them."

Audubon objected to this arrangement, and proposed to lay on his blanket by the fire; but they would not for a moment permit this, and the debate was settled by their carrying out their own plan, taking to the floor, and yielding the bed to the guests.

The weather was bad in the morning, and the host with great earnestness, seconded by the entreaties of his wife, pressed them to remain; and when they insisted on going, provided a hearty breakfast for them, and, on horseback, piloted them back to the road, which they had lost. Not a penny would he receive for the entertainment, but bade them adieu with a smile, hoping that some other fortunate mistake would bring them again under his roof.

THE EARTHQUAKE.

While traveling one afternoon through what was then called the "barrens" of Kentucky, in the month of November, jogging along on horseback, he remarked a sudden and strange darkness rising from the western horizon. Accustomed as he was to sudden and heavy thunder-storms, he took but little notice of the clouds, only encouraging the speed of his horse in order to reach the shelter of a friend's house, not far distant.

before the rain should come in torrents. After riding about a mile, he imagined that he heard the distant rumbling of the coming tornado, and spurred his horse to still greater speed; but much to his surprise, instead of moving faster the horse nearly stopped, and began to place one foot after another as carefully upon the ground as if he were walking upon a sheet of ice. Audubon thought he had suddenly broken down, and was on the point of dismounting to lead him, when suddenly he fell, groaning piteously. He hung down his head, spread out his fore legs, as if to save himself from falling, and then remained perfectly quiet, groaning all the time. He thought his horse was about to die, and was on the point of springing from his back, when, in an instant, all the shrubs and trees began to move from their very roots, the ground rose and fell in successive furrows, like the waters of the sea, and it broke upon him, to his dismay, that he was experiencing the shocks of a severe earthquake. The instinct of his horse had apprehended sooner than himself the nature of the commotion around them. He had heard and read of earthquakes, but no words could express the sensations he then experienced. He found himself rocking upon his horse, like a child in a cradle, expecting every moment the ground would open and engulf them both. The fearful convulsion lasted only a few minutes, and the heavens again brightened as quickly as they had become obscured. His horse at once raised his head, rose upon his feet, and galloped off as lively as if without a rider. Not being without apprehension that the shock might have been more severe at his own house, he hurried as rapidly as his steed could carry him, and discovered to his comfort that no harm had occurred, and that his family had only felt alarmed in reference to his safety.

The earthquake, however, was not over. Shock succeeded shock almost every day and night for several weeks. Strange to say, they became so used to it as to cease almost to notice it. On one of these occasions he was at a friend's house attending a truly western wedding, the guests coming from a distance, and remaining all night with their host.

They were in a log-house of large dimensions, and solidly built. The host was a physician, and had his surgical instruments and bottles of medicine arranged on shelves in one corner of the house. It was late when they retired, and as morning began to dawn, the rumbling noise preceding the earthquake began so loudly as to arouse every inmate from slumber, and to drive them in great consternation from their beds. Every person, old and young, filled with alarm at the creaking of the log-house, and apprehending its instant destruction, rushed wildly in their sleeping garments to the inclosure in front of the dwelling. The earth waved like a field of corn before the breeze, and the birds left their perches and flew about, apparently in great distress. The doctor, anxious in reference to his perishable jars of medicine, rushed into his shop-room, and tried to prevent their dancing off the shelves to the floor. He spread out his arms and jumped vigorously about the front of the cases, pushing them back here and there; but with so little success, that before the shock was over he had lost nearly all he possessed. The earthquakes produced more serious consequences in other places. Near New Madrid, and for some distance on the Mississippi, the earth was rent asunder in several places, one or two islands sunk forever, and the inhabitants fled in dismay toward the eastern shores.

THE TORNADO.

There is another sublime exhibition of the power of the great Creator in the elements which he has created, and which he alone holds in his hand, of common occurrence in this western world. Audubon thus describes his personal experience of a tornado. He had left the village of Shawaney, situated upon the banks of the Ohio. The weather was very pleasant. His horse was jogging quietly along. He had just forded Highland Creek, and was entering upon a tract of interval land, called bottom land, lying between it and Canoe Creek, when suddenly he remarked a great difference in the appearance of the heavens. A thick haze overspread the country, and for some time he expected an earthquake. His horse, however, with unerring instinct, gave none of the accustomed signs of such an occurrence. At the edge of the valley, he stopped at a brook to quench his thirst. He was leaning on his knees, with his lips near the water, when he heard a distant murmuring sound of an

extraordinary nature. After drinking, as he
arose, and looked toward the south-west, he
observed a yellowish oval spot, differing
from anything he had ever seen before.
Little time was left him for consideration,
as the next moment a smart breeze began
to disturb the taller trees. It soon increased
to an unaccustomed height, and soon the
smaller branches were seen falling in a slanting direction to the ground. Two minutes
had scarcely elapsed, when the whole forest
before him was in a fearful motion. Trees
were pressed against each other with a
creaking noise. Turning toward the direction from which the wind blew, he saw, to
his astonishment, the noblest trees of the
forest bending their lofty heads for a while,
and then, unable to stand against the blast,
snapping with a crash like thunder. So
rapid was the progress of the storm, that
before he could think of taking measures for
his safety, the hurricane was passing opposite
to the place where he stood. "Never," he
says, " can I forget the scene which at that
moment presented itself. The tops of the
trees were seen moving in the strangest
manner, in the central current of the tempest, which carried along with it a mingled

mass of twigs and foliage that completely obscured the view. Some of the largest trees were seen bending and writhing under the gale; others suddenly snapped across; and many after a momentary resistance fell, uprooted, to the earth. The mass of branches, twigs, foliage, and dust that moved through the air was whirled onward like a cloud of feathers, and on passing, disclosed a wide space filled with fallen trees, naked stumps, and heaps of shapeless ruins, which marked the path of the tempest. This space was about a fourth of a mile in breadth, and to my imagination resembled the dried up bed of the Mississippi, with its thousands of planters and sawyers,* strewed in the sand and inclined in various degrees. The horrible noise resembled that of the great cataracts of Niagara, and as it howled along in the track of the desolating tempest, it produced a feeling in my mind which it is impossible to describe. The principal force of the hurricane was now over, although millions of twigs and small branches, that had been brought from a great distance, were

* These are immense trees with one end firmly fixed in the bed of the river, and the other either quietly protruding above the water, or swaying with the current.

5

seen following the blast, as if drawn onward
by some mysterious power. They floated in
the air for some hours after, as if supported
by the thick mass of dust that rose high
above the ground. The sky had now a
greenish, lurid hue, and an extremely dis-
agreeable sulphureous odor was diffused in
the atmosphere. I waited in amazement,
having sustained no material injury, until nature at length assumed her wonted aspect."

He was obliged to lead his horse by the
bridle, to enable him to leap the fallen trees,
while he scrambled under or over them as
best he could. In other portions of its path
across the country the tornado had over-
turned houses, and caught up animals, and
even human beings, in its course. A cow
was found lodged in the fork of a half brok-
en tree. Audubon crossed the path of the
storm afterward seven hundred miles from
the point where he personally experienced its
fury. It seemed to have swept along its
whole course a path about a quarter of a
mile wide.

"AN ODD FISH."

Audubon's adventures were not only connected with strange events in the natural

world, but often with singular individuals. "What an odd-looking fellow," said Audubon to himself one day as, walking by the river, he observed a man landing from a boat, with what seemed to be a bundle of dried clover upon his back. He hurried up the bank, while the boatmen stared at the grotesque figure he cut, and addressing him, asked if he would point out the residence of Mr. Audubon. "I am the man," was the answer, "and will gladly lead you to my dwelling."

The man rubbed his hands together with delight, and, without any remark, handed him a letter. It was from a friend, and contained only the amusing sentence :

"My dear Audubon, I send you an odd fish, which you may prove to be undescribed, and hope you will do so in your next letter."

Not apprehending the meaning at once, Mr. Audubon innocently asked, turning to the individual, where the odd fish was. The gentleman smiled, rubbed his hands, and with the greatest good-humor, remarked that he presumed his friend referred to him under the title of an odd fish. Mr. Audubon, somewhat confounded by his own stupidity, could only stammer out an apology.

When they reached the house, Mr. Audubon ordered the servant to go to the boat for the gentleman's baggage; but he at once assured him that he had only what was upon his back. He then loosened his pack of weeds, pulled off his shoes, and while engaged in drawing off his stockings, taking special care to cover the holes about the heels, he related in the liveliest manner his late adventures. He had walked a great distance, had only taken passage in the *ark* across the river, and was sorry that his garments were so much the worse for wear. He refused an offer of clean clothes, and somewhat reluctantly accepted water, to render his hands and face more presentable at dinner. He wore a long, loose, yellow nankeen coat, much injured by use, and stained all over with the juice of plants. He had a waistcoat of the same material, with enormous pockets, buttoning to the chin, and hanging over his pantaloons. The latter were made tight, and buttoned round his ankles. His beard was very long, and his lank black hair hung loosely over his shoulders. He had a high, broad forehead, and when he spoke gave evidence of strong mental powers.

He informed Mr. Audubon that he had

come expressly to see his drawings, as he had been told that he accompanied his representations of birds with truthful sketches of plants and shrubs found in the same localities. He was impatient at once to see his portfolios. When his eye chanced to fall upon one quite new to him, he looked at it carefully, shook his head, and remarked that no such plant existed in nature. Mr. Audubon quietly remarked that it was common in the immediate neighborhood, and that he would show it to him on the morrow.

"But why to-morrow?" was the impatient response; "let us go now."

They went out together, and when, on the river bank, Mr. Audubon pointed out the plant, the Frenchman, for such he was, seemed fairly to be beside himself over it.

"He plucked the plants one after another, danced, hugged me in his arms, and exultingly told me that he had found not merely a new species, but a new genus. When we returned home the naturalist opened the bundle which he had brought on his back, and took out a journal, rendered water-proof by means of a leather case, examined the new plant, and wrote its description."

It is from the self-denying labors of such

men as these that our works on science are collected. We, in our pleasant homes and schools, enjoy the results of thousands of miles of travel and of the most careful study. His criticisms upon the drawings of Audubon were of great service to him, from his knowledge both of nature and of books. The Frenchman would only believe what he saw with his own eyes. The light of the candle, the windows being open, attracted many insects, among which was a large species of the beetle, the scientific name of which is scarabæus. Audubon caught one, and assured the naturalist that it was so strong that it could crawl upon the table with the candlestick upon its back.

"I should like to *see* the experiment made," was his immediate response. Accordingly, the insect was placed underneath the candlestick, causing it constantly to change its position, until, coming upon the edge of the table, it dropped upon the floor, and taking to its wings made its escape.

Very late at night the Frenchman was shown to his room. All had retired in the house. Mr. Audubon supposed all to be asleep but himself, when suddenly he heard a great uproar in the room given to the naturalist. Mr. Audubon hurried to the door, and, to his astonishment, found his guest nude and running about the room, holding the handle of his favorite violin, the body of which he had battered to pieces against the wall, attempting to kill the bats which had entered the open window, attracted by the light. Mr. Audubon stood amazed, as the man continued jumping around until he was fairly exhausted; when he begged him to procure him one of the animals, as he was confident that it was a new species. This Mr. Audubon soon succeeded in doing. The struggle over, he bade him good-night once more, leaving him in the room, now perfectly strewed with his scattered plants. The Frenchman noticed the curious look with which he surveyed the confusion.

"Never mind," said he, "never mind. I'll soon arrange them again. I have the bat, and that's enough."

They passed a number of days in their several occupations; the Frenchman searching for plants, and Audubon for birds. One day, as Mr. Audubon returned, wet and bespattered with mud, from a hunt in a cane-brake, his guest expressed a desire to be shown the interior of one of these places, as

he had never visited one. The cane formerly grew spontaneously over great portions
of Kentucky, but the introduction of cattle
and horses, who greatly relish them, together
with cultivation, has caused it rapidly to
disappear. It grows to a height of from
twelve to thirty feet, and is from one to
two inches in diameter. The plants grow
close together, and becoming tangled, present an almost impenetrable thicket. Wild
beasts make their haunts here, and to follow the bear or the cougar through these
retreats is a labor of peculiar difficulty and
danger. The hunters often cut little paths
through the thickets with their knives; but
the usual mode of passing through is by
pushing one's self backward, and thus wedg-
ing a way between the stems.

Having fixed a day, after an early breakfast they started for the cane-brake. For a
time they proceeded without much difficulty,
Audubon leading the way, and cutting the
cane as he advanced. Soon the path became
more tangled; they were obliged to turn
their backs to the foe and push forward in
that way as best they might. The naturalist stopped now and then to pluck and
examine a plant. After a time they came

No. 728.

Audubon and the Odd Fish in the Cane-brake.

upon a fallen tree, which so obstructed their passage that, instead of attempting to push themselves through its branches and over it, they were just on the eve of going round it, when from the center of the tangled mass out rushed a bear, bursting aside the canes with great force and snuffing the air in a frightful manner. The poor Frenchman was suddenly terror-struck, and in his haste to escape made a desperate attempt to run. He was soon, however, perfectly and help-lessly pinioned by the canes. His terrible fright and his ridiculous position were al-most too much for Audubon, and he could hardly refrain from laughter. It was aid, however, and not a laugh at his expense, that the somewhat irritated naturalist now loudly demanded. He would have been glad to have retraced his way to the point of starting; but as Audubon wished him to have a clear idea of a cane-brake, now that the bear had disappeared, he persuaded him to advance, as the worst difficulties were probably conquered.

The way, however, became more tangled, and a dark, heavy cloud began to gather over them. The poor naturalist, unused to such adventures, panted, perspired, and seemed quite overcome with 'fatigue. The thunder now began to rumble, and soon the rain fell in floods. The withered particles of leaves and bark attached to the canes stuck to their clothes. They were scratched by briars, and now and then bitterly tormented by nettles. The Frenchman seriously inquired if there was any hope of their getting alive out of the horrible situation in which they were. Audubon begged him to be patient and take courage, as deliverance would eventually come, although at this time he knew that two more miles of this struggling work were to be accomplished. The Frenchman threw away all his plants, emptied his full pockets of all their specimens of natural history, and thus lightened, commenced his terrible task afresh.

It was long after midday before they reached the banks of the river. Audubon blew his horn, and a boat came to their rescue.

The Frenchman remained several days longer with him, adding to his collections, but never again expressing a desire to enter a cane-brake. One evening at tea, when he was expected to join the family, he could not be found. His specimens were found to

have been all removed from his room.
They spent the night in searching the neighborhood for him, but in vain. Some weeks
afterward a letter was received from him in
a distant place, conveying his thanks for the
attentions he had received.

DANIEL BOONE.

Among all the eccentric and noted characters that Audubon met during his wanderings over the wild lands of the western
region at this period of his life, (about 1810,)
there was no one more marked in his character, nor one who left a stronger impression of himself upon that portion of our
country, than Daniel Boone, or, as he was
usually called, Colonel Boone.

Mr. Audubon once passed the night under the same roof with him. They had been
hunting together, and during the excursion
the colonel's extraordinary skill with his rifle
had been fully explained. The colonel was
one of the first settlers in Kentucky, the
leader of all the early, hardy emigrants in
their fierce encounters with the wild beasts
and the wilder Indians, who, up to the entrance of the white men into the country, had

been the undisputed proprietors of the soil.
Colonel Boone was a giant in stature, with a
broad and prominent chest; every limb displayed muscular strength in its perfection.
His countenance exhibited enterprise, courage, and perseverance. Every word he ut-
tered bore the mark of unqualified truth.
Our young readers will be gratified to obtain some one of the biographies of this truly great as well as eccentric man, and read
the strange adventures through which he
passed.

When night came, at this meeting between
him and Audubon, the latter undressed to
lay down for the night; but Boone merely
removed his hunting shirt, and arranged a
few folds of blankets on the floor, remarking
that he preferred to lay there rather than upon the softest bed. Before they dropped
asleep Boone related to his companion the
following incident from his life.

He was hunting, he said, on the banks of
the Green river, at a time when the lower
part of Kentucky was only inhabited by the
native possessors of the soil. The emigrants
from Virginia, under his leadership, had been
waging war with them. He had himself,
he said, followed their tracks through the

woods as he would the path of a ravenous
animal. By such a relentless war as this the
red men were driven from their homes. It
is not surprising that they often turned upon
their pursuers with the ferocity of wild
beasts, and spared from their tomahawks
neither women nor children. One dark night,
Boone went on to relate, the Indians out-
witted him, and he was suddenly made a
prisoner. The stratagem had been managed
with great skill on the part of the Indians.
No sooner had Boone extinguished the fire
of his camp, and laid down in perfect securi-
ty, as he thought, to rest, than he felt himself seized by a large number of hands, the individuals to whom they belonged not being
distinguishable in the darkness. They confined him at once, so that he could not move.
It was vain to resist, so he quietly resigned
himself to his fate, having but little doubt as
to what that fate would be. They removed
him a few miles distant from his camp, without a word of complaint on his part, a course
that served to impress the Indians favorably,
as it showed them that Boone was as fearless
of death as themselves. When the Indian
camp was reached, the sight of Boone, who
had been considered their mortal enemy, and

whose unerring rifle had laid many of their tribe in the dust, caused inexpressible delight. Boone remained perfectly speechless, simply meditating some plan of escape.

The women fell to searching his clothing, and in his hunting-shirt found a flask filled with very strong whisky. A terrific grin, he said, was exhibited on their murderous countenances at this discovery, and Boone could only heartily wish it might accomplish their intoxication, for now the first glimmer of a hope of escape dawned upon him. The whole troop immediately began to drink, passing the bottle from mouth to mouth, beating their chests and shouting out their songs. Boone noticed, to his sorrow, that the women drank more than the warriors, and he was just beginning to despair, when the report of a gun was heard in the distance. The Indians immediately leaped upon their feet. The singing and drinking closed at once. The men walked off some distance, talking with the squaws. (Indian wives.) He knew they were consulting about himself, and concluded that the Indians would go themselves to discover the occasion of the firing so near their camp, and leave their prisoner under the guard of the women

And so it turned out. The men took their guns and walked away; the squaws sat down again, and immediately commenced their attentions afresh upon the whisky flask. With pleasure did Boone see them becoming more and more drunk, until finally they were perfectly stupefied by it. They rolled about a while, then began to snore in their drunken sleep. He had no other means of freeing himself from the cords that bound him than by rolling over and over toward the fire; he finally succeeded in burning them asunder. He rose on his feet, stretched his stiffened limbs, snatched up his rifle, and for once refrained from taking the life of Indians when in his power. It looked, he said, so much like murder to slaughter those helpless victims of drunkenness that he put aside the temptation and hastened away.

The singular portion of the story follows. He determined to mark the spot, and going to a thrifty young ash-tree he cut out of it three large chips and ran off. He soon crossed Green river, and burying himself in the intricacies of the cane-brake, he placed himself beyond the danger of pursuit. It had been twenty years since this happened, and five years since he had been in that portion of the country.   He probably never would have gone there again had he not been summoned as a witness in a lawsuit, involving that very tract of land where this adventure occurred. A gentleman had moved from Virginia, and having a large tract of land granted to him, had laid claim to a portion adjoining Green river, on one of the corners of which was the ash-tree on which Boone had made his mark. He had finished his survey, beginning, as the deed read, at " an ash-tree marked by three distinct notches of the tomahawk of a white man."   The tree had grown very much, and the bark had long covered the marks; but the gentleman had, from some source, heard the story of Boone's adventures with the Indians, and wrote to him, thinking it possible that he might be able to aid them in fixing upon the tree referred to in the deed, the marks of which were no longer discoverable. After a little reflection the whole scene with the Indians came to his recollection, and he thought he could go directly to the spot. They mounted their horses (Boone and interested party) and started for the Green River Bottoms, so called.   Great changes had taken place in twenty years.   At last he found the spot where he crossed the river, and waiting for the moon to rise, he started in the direction in which it seemed to him the ash could be reached. As he approached the place the scene became more real to him. It almost seemed to him that he must find the Indians still there. They camped near the spot and waited until day. At the rising of the sun Boone was on foot, and after much thought concluded the ash-tree then in sight must be the very one bearing his marks.

"Well, Colonel Boone," said the gentleman, "if you think so I hope it may prove true, but we must have some witnesses; do you remain here while I go and bring some of the settlers whom I know."

Boone passed the time of his absence in rambling about to see if any deer still remained in the vicinity. But what a change had these years effected! At the time of his Indian adventure he could not have walked in any direction a mile without meeting a buck or a bear. There were thousands of buffaloes on the hills of Kentucky; but as he now wandered for the last time upon the banks of Green river not a deer was to be seen. Three gentlemen soon rode up as witnesses. Boone took an ax from one of them
6

and cut a few chips off the bark. No signs were yet to be seen. So he cut again until he thought it was time to be cautious, and he then scraped away with his knife until three notches were as plainly visible as if they had been cut the day before. The gentlemen were astonished. Boone made his statement of the facts in their presence, and the party interested, upon this testimony, obtained his suit in court.

THE RUNAWAY SLAVE.

We record one more of the adventures of Audubon during his long and laborious excursions in the wilds, because such events will now, thanks to a divine Providence overruling the awful civil war at this time pending, become rare, if not impossible. Such scenes have been the common incidents of swamp expeditions, and thousands of such poor, terror-stricken hearts have beaten wildly in the intricacies of dismal and unhealthy marshes. The event made a powerful impression upon the mind of Audubon.

It was late in the afternoon of a sultry day, when the atmosphere of a Louisiana swamp is laden with poisonous effluvia, and he had started for his distant lodgings, loaded with five or six wood ibises and a heavy gun, which prevented him from moving with much speed. He reached the banks of a miry bayou (a creek of water, jutting far into the land from the river) only a few yards in breadth, but of which, on account of its muddiness, he could not ascertain the depth. Lest the weight of his burden might sink him, he first threw to the opposite bank his birds and his gun; and drawing his hunting-knife to defend himself from the alligators, he entered the stream with his faithful dog Plato. The water and mire were deep, but after a short struggle he reached the shore. He had hardly touched the opposite bank and brought himself erect, when his dog rushed to him, exhibiting marks of terror, and pouring forth a stifled growl. Supposing this was produced by the scent or sight of a bear or wolf, Audubon stooped to take up his gun, when a powerful voice commanded him to "stand still or die!" Such a challenge in the woods was entirely unexpected. He instantly raised and cocked his gun, although, as yet, he did not see the person whose voice he had heard. Presently a tall, firmly-built negro emerged from the thick underbrush, and with a still louder voice repeated the same command. Audubon could readily have terminated his life by touching the lock of his gun, already cocked; but noticing that the gun which the negro pointed at his breast was a wretched rusty piece, he thought he had nothing to fear. So he brought his gun to his side, and tapping his dog quietly, he asked the man what he wanted. The gentleness of Audubon subdued the negro and allayed his fears.

"Master," said he, "I am a runaway. I might, perhaps, have shot you down; but God forbid it, for I feel just now as if I saw him ready to pass his judgment against me for such a foul deed, and I ask mercy at your hands. For God's sake do not kill me, master!"

Audubon immediately quieted him, and asked him why he had left his quarters, as he must certainly have fared better there than in this unwholesome swamp.

"Master," said the slave, "my story is a short but a sorrowful one. My camp is close by, and as I know you cannot reach home to-night, if you will follow me there, depend upon *my honor* you shall be safe until the morning, when I will carry your birds, if you choose, to the great road."

The large, intelligent eyes of the negro, his calm self-possession, and his apparent manliness, assured Audubon that it was safe to trust the honor of his sable acquaintance. He told him to go on, and he would *follow him*. The negro noticed the emphasis laid on these last words, and seemed to understand their meaning so thoroughly that he at once said:

"There, master, take my butcher's knife, while I throw away the flint and priming from my gun!"

Audubon says: "I felt confounded; this was too much for me; I refused the knife, and told him to keep his piece ready, in case we might accidentally meet a cougar or a bear."

The man offered him his hand. "Master," said he, "I beg your thanks," and the negro gave him a squeeze that impressed him both with the goodness of his heart, and the immense power of his hand.

After moving on through the woods at some distance, crossing several bayous, at every one of which the negro first threw over his knife and gun, and then waited unarmed until Audubon had crossed, they finally came to the borders of an immense cane-brake, where Audubon had heretofore killed several deer. Through this they had to creep, often on all fours, as best they might. The negro led the way, dividing the tangled stalks, and always insisting on aiding Audubon over when they reached a fallen tree. He was a perfect Indian in his knowledge of the woods, for he kept a direct course as precisely as any "Redskin." Suddenly he gave a loud shriek, not unlike that of an owl. Audubon, surprised, involuntarily raised his gun.

"No harm, master," said the negro; "I only gave notice to my wife and children that I am coming."

A tremulous cry of the same character soon came back from the recesses of the forest. "The runaway's lips," says Audubon, "separated with an expression of gentleness and delight, when his beautiful set of ivory teeth seemed to smile through the dusk of evening that was thickening around us. 'Master,' said he, 'my wife, though black, is as beautiful to me as the president's wife is to him; she is my queen, and I look on our young ones as so many princes; but

N 7-8

Audubon at the Camp of the Runaway.

you shall see them all, for here they are, thank God!'"

In the center of the cane-brake he found a regular camp. A small fire was burning, and on the coals were large slices of venison. A boy nine or ten years old was blowing the ashes from some fine sweet potatoes. The wife did not raise her eyes to Audubon, and the three smaller children retired into a corner, as if affrighted at the sight of a stranger. The negro told them that their visitor was a friend. Audubon's clothes were hung to dry, and his gun was carefully cleaned; while his dog, that at once became the favorite of the children, was made well contented by a large piece of deer's flesh. The venison and potatoes looked tempting, and at their invitation the guest drew up and made as hearty a meal as ever in his life. After supper both husband and wife seemed anxious to tell him their story, and to seek his aid.

About eighteen months before, it appeared, a planter residing not far from the swamp, having met with losses, was obliged to sell some of his slaves. The negro, being well-known as a valuable slave, brought a large sum, and his wife, who was offered separately,

was bidden off by another party for a great
price. The children were bought by still
other families. The wife was carried away
a hundred miles from her husband, and the
children were distributed in different places.
The man pined for his wife and children
until he refrained from food and became
sick. On a stormy night the poor negro
made his escape, and being well acquainted
with the surrounding country, plunged into
the recesses of the cane-brake, where his
camp was now situated. A few nights after·
ward he found the abode of his wife and led
her away to the swamp, and from time to
time he succeeded in drawing away from
their distant homes his children one at a
time. But now the painful task was to provide for his helpless ones, while all the surrounding country was ransacked by the
planters in search of the runaways. The
dark night when others slept was his only
opportunity. He prowled around his old
master's habitation, and the servants, among
whom he had been a favorite, would load
him with supplies. He finally found a gun,
and having obtained ammunition, he ventured
during the day to hunt around his camp. It
was while thus engaged that he had fallen

upon Audubon. As they finished the story both rose from their seat with eyes full of tears, and sobbed out, "Good master, for God's sake, do something for us and our children." Their little children were lying around asleep in fearless innocence. "Who," says Audubon, "could have heard such a tale without emotion? I promised them my most cordial assistance. They both sat up that night to watch my repose, and I slept close to their urchins, as if on a bed of the softest down."

In the morning Audubon persuaded them to take their children and accompany him to their first master. Audubon happened to be well acquainted with him. They were cordially received upon the plantation. The master repurchased them from their owners, and afterward treated them with his previous kindness. Audubon remarks of them, "that they were rendered as happy *as slaves generally are* in that country." How happy a condition this can be, exposed to all the uncertainties of business, and liable to have all the family relations suddenly and forever sundered, even among the kindest masters, can be readily imagined.

CHAPTER VI.

AUDUBON'S STUDIES IN NATURAL HISTORY.

The adventures recorded in the previous chapter, with many others of the same description, employed but a small portion of his time, and occurred when he was engaged in pursuits of far greater interest and importance. These travels over so many weary miles, through forests and prairie, among wild Indians, and often wilder white settlers, were not simply expeditions for pleasure, or excursions for hunting and adventures. During all these years of wandering Audubon had one object, and that was, to become thoroughly acquainted with the appearance and habits of all the principal birds of our country, and to draw from nature a perfect and full-size picture of them.

In five large closely printed volumes, entitled "Ornithological Biography," which are full of interest from the commencement to the close, Audubon has given a description of over four hundred different species of birds. That our young readers may have some idea of the pleasure which the study of natural history will afford them, of the truly valuable results of a long life which many of the unwise friends of Audubon thought to have been almost thrown away, because it was not devoted to the accumulation of money, and more especially to direct their minds to the wonderful exhibition of the power, wisdom, and love of God in creation, we devote one chapter to a few of the many interesting descriptions contained in Audubon's volumes. The whole work will be found in the public libraries; and in all the bookstores very entertaining volumes both upon birds and beasts, gleaned from the works of such laborers in the field as Audubon, may be obtained. Chiefly to inspire a taste for such reading has this biography been undertaken.

THE WILD TURKEY.

One of the largest and most valuable native birds of North America is the wild turkey. It has been domesticated, and become one of the most important of the barn-

yard fowls, but still is found in immense
flocks, in the wild state, in the western and
southern portions of our country, where
only the emigrant has as yet raised his cabin.
About the beginning of October, when
scarcely any seeds or fruits have fallen from
the trees, the turkeys begin to assemble in
flocks, and gradually to move toward the
rich bottom lands of the Mississippi and its
tributaries. The males, commonly called
gobblers, associate in parties of from ten to
a hundred, and search for food apart from
the females; while the latter are seen advancing singly, each with its brood of young,
then about two thirds grown, or sometimes
they associate in parties, containing several
families, amounting to seventy or eighty
birds. They very carefully shun the males,
who are apt to destroy their young broods,
even after they have attained some size, by
repeated blows upon the head. Old and
young move forward on foot, only taking
wing when their progress is stopped by a
river, or they are startled by a hunter's dog.
When they come to a river they betake
themselves to the highest eminences, and
there often remain a whole day, and sometimes longer, apparently for purposes of con-

sultation. During this time the males are heard gobbling, calling, and making much ado. They may be seen strutting about, as if striving to raise their courage to the demands of the occasion. Even the females take upon themselves some portion of this pompous bearing, spreading out their tails, running around each other, *purring* loudly, and performing extravagant leaps. At length, when the weather appears settled, and all around is quiet, the whole flock flies to the tops of the highest trees, when, at the signal of a single *chuck* given by the leader, it rises into the air and takes flight for the opposite shore. The old and fat birds easily get over, even if the river is a mile in breadth; but the younger and weaker often fall into the water. Nature, however, has fully prepared them for this. When they strike the water they bring their wings close to their body, spread out their tail as a support, stretch forward their neck, and striking out with their legs, swim with great vigor toward the shore. It is remarked, that after thus crossing a large stream, they ramble about for some time as if bewildered. In this state they easily fall a prey to the hunter.

When the turkey arrives in parts where

the *mast*, is abundant, (which is not merely the nut of the beech, but a general name for all kinds of forest fruits and berries,) they separate into smaller flocks, composed of birds of different ages and both sexes, and commence devouring all before them. This occurs about the middle of November. They become so gentle after these long journeys as often to approach the settler's cabin and associate with the domestic fowl. They pass the remainder of the fall and part of the winter in roaming through the forests and feeding chiefly upon the mast. By the middle of February they begin to unite in pairs once more. The female utters a call note, and all the gobblers within hearing return the sound, rolling note after note very rapidly, much after the manner of the domestic turkey when an unexpected noise or presence disturbs him. If the female be upon the ground, all the males immediately fly toward the spot, and whether the hen is in sight or not, spread out and erect their tail, draw the head back on the shoulders, depress their wings with a quivering motion, strut pompously about, and emit a succession of puffs from the lungs, stopping now and then to listen and look.

While thus occupied the males often en counter each other, in which case desperate battles take place, often ending in the loss of life, the weaker falling under repeated blows administered upon the head by the stronger. After an acquaintance is formed the hen follows its favorite male, roosting near and often upon the same tree, until she commences to lay, when she avoids his company most of the time, in order to save her eggs, which he would break if he could find them. They begin to lay about the middle of April, the hen searching for a dry place in which to deposit her eggs. She finds the most secluded position possible, in order to avoid the eye of the crow, as that bird often watches the turkey when going to her nest, and remains in the neighborhood until after she leaves, that he may rob and eat the eggs The nest is a hollow, scooped out in the ground by the side of a log, or in a thicket or cane-brake in some dry place, and is lined with dry leaves. The eggs are of a dull cream color, sprinkled with red dots; sometimes they amount to twenty, although usually they number from ten to fifteen. When about to lay an egg, the hen approaches the nest with the utmost caution, scarcely ever taking the same course twice. When she leaves the nest she covers the eggs over carefully with leaves, so that it is very difficult to find it. For the same reason they prefer islands in the rivers for depositing their eggs and rearing their young. When a person approaches within sight of a female while laying or sitting she never moves, unless she knows that she has been discovered, but crouches lower until the person has passed. They never go near a nest again if they find that a snake or any other animal has been to it and sucked any of the eggs. Several hens have been known to associate together for mutual protection, deposit their eggs in the same nest, and raise their broods together.

Audubon once found three sitting upon forty-two eggs. In such cases the common nest is always watched by one of the hens, so that no crow, raven, nor even pole-cat, dares approach it. The mother will not leave her eggs when near hatching under any circumstances while life remains. She will even allow an inclosure to be made around her, and thus suffer imprisonment rather than abondon them. Audubon says:

"I once witnessed the hatching of a brood

of turkeys, which I watched for the purpose
of securing them, together with the parent.
I concealed myself on the ground within a
very few feet, and saw her raise herself half
the length of her legs, look anxiously upon
the eggs, cluck with a sound peculiar to the
mother on such occasions, carefully remove
each half-empty shell, and with her bill
caress and dry the young birds, that already
stood tottering, and attempting to make
their way out of the nest. Yes, I have seen
this, and have left mother and young to better care than mine could have proved, to the
care of their Creator and mine. I have seen
them all emerge from the shell, and in a
few moments after tumble, roll, and push
each other forward, with astonishing and in-
scrutable instinct."

Before leaving the nest with her brood,
the mother shakes herself, arranges her
feathers, and quite spruces up for the occasion. She turns her eyes in every direction,
stretching out her neck to discover if there
are any hawks or other enemies around,
spreads her wings a little as she walks, and
with a gentle cluck keeps her little flock close
to her. They frequently return the first
night to the nest. They then remove to

some distance, keeping on high ground, the mother dreading wet weather, which is extremely dangerous to the young, when only covered with a soft hairy down. If once completely wetted they seldom recover. To prevent the effects of a chill from rain, the mother will often pluck the buds of the spice-wood bush, and give them to her young.

In about a fortnight the young birds, which had previously rested upon the ground, leave it and fly to some large, low branch of a tree, sheltering themselves on either side of the mother under her widely extended wings.

The most formidable enemies of the turkey, after man, are the lynx and the owl. The lynx sucks their eggs, and is extremely expert in seizing both the young and the old. When he has discovered a flock of turkeys, he will follow them at a distance for some time, until he discovers the direction in which they are proceeding. He then makes a rapid circular movement, gets in advance of the flock, and lays himself down in ambush. When the birds come up, he springs upon one in a moment, and makes off with him, to enjoy his stolen meal.

They manage often to escape from the

large species of the owl, which is an especial
enemy to them. The turkeys roost in flocks
on naked branches of trees. The owls,
on their night excursions, discover them, and
hover around, watching a favorable opportunity to strike their prey. Their approach
is generally discovered, and a single cluck
arouses the whole flock. They all start up
on their legs, and watch the owl. Soon selecting a victim, he glances down upon it
like an arrow. But the turkey, on the alert,
lowers its head and spreads its tail over its
back, so that the bill of the owl is met by a
smooth, inclined surface, along which it slides
without the least injury to the turkey. The
night robber turns away discomfited without his expected victim.

Sometimes turkeys give the settlers considerable trouble, resorting to the cornfields
when the crop just makes its appearance
above the soil, and destroying great quanti-
ties of it. This of course cannot be permitted, and the ingenuity of the farmer is taxed
to deliver himself from their encroachments.
One who had thus suffered cut a long trench
in a favorable situation, put a quantity of
corn in it, and having heavily loaded a famous duck gun of his, placed it so that he

could pull the trigger by means of a string, in a position quite concealed from the birds. The turkeys soon discovered the corn and rapidly dispatched it. He filled the trench again, and one day when he saw it quite black with birds he whistled loudly: every head was raised. He suddenly pulled the string, the gun exploded, the living turkeys took to their legs and made wonderful time toward the prairie; nine fell victims to their appetites. The turkeys never troubled that field again. What was it that kept them away?

When Audubon lived in Henderson he tamed a young male turkey, having caught it when it was only two or three days old. It would follow any person who called it, and became quite a favorite in the village. It never would roost with the tame turkeys, but always at night flew to the roof of the house. When two years old it began to fly to the woods, where it remained during the day, but returned at night. In the succeeding spring it changed its roost to a high cottonwood-tree on the banks of the Ohio. One morning it flew off at a very early hour to the woods, and did not return again. Sometime after Audubon was hunting near some small lakes adjoining Green river, when he saw a fine large gobbler cross the path before him, moving leisurely along. He ordered his dog to chase it. Juno rushed toward it with great rapidity, but to his surprise the turkey paid no attention to him. The dog was on the point of seizing the bird, when she suddenly stopped and hurried toward her master. Audubon hastened forward, and to his surprise recognized his pet turkey. It had discovered the dog and would not fly from her, and the dog evidently recognized an old acquaintance. The bird was carried home, and remained until it was accidentally shot the next spring. What was it in this bird that enabled it to recognize in this dog an old friend, and induced it to quietly await the coming of its former master?

How wonderfully has our common Creator adapted every living thing to its appropriate place, and supplied every creature with the means of providing for its own wants. This is only one bird of a thousand, and yet who, reading the records of its life and habits, can doubt that the hand that fashioned it was divine?

> " The birds, that rise on quiv'ring wing,
>   Proclaim their Maker's praise,
> And all the mingling sounds of spring
>   To Thee an anthem raise."

THE BIRD OF WASHINGTON.

To one of the largest and noblest of the eagle species, first described by himself, Audubon gave the appropriate name of "The Bird of Washington." His first view of this powerful bird was obtained under the following circumstances: He was prosecuting a trading voyage on the Upper Mississippi in the month of February, 1814. Keen wintry winds whistled by them, and there was little in the chilling aspect around to awaken interest. His eye was chiefly attracted by the multitudes of ducks of different species, and the vast flocks of swans which, from time to time, passed them. His trading companion was a Canadian who had been for many years engaged in the fur trade. Seeing Audubon's curiosity aroused by the birds, he seemed anxious to find new objects to divert him. An eagle flew over them.

"How fortunate," he exclaimed; "this is what I could have wished. Look, sir! the Great Eagle, and the only one I have ever seen since I left the lakes."

Audubon was instantly on his feet observing it, and from its appearance then conclud-

ed that it was a species he had never seen
before. The trader assured him that the
birds were rare; that they sometimes followed hunters to feed upon the remains of
the animals they slew, when the lakes were
frozen over ; but when these were open they
obtained their food by diving into the water
like the fish hawk.

From this time Audubon felt a strong de
sire to discover one of these birds, and to
learn more in reference to its habits.

A few years after this, while fishing upon
Green river, near its junction with the Ohio,
and where the river was bordered for some
distance by a range of very high cliffs, he
observed on the rocks, which were at that
place nearly perpendicular, a quantity of
white guano, which he attributed to the
presence of owls. Mentioning the circumstance to a companion who lived in the vicinity, he told him the place was the resort
of the white-headed eagle. But Audubon
knew too well the habit of this bird, and remarked that it never built its nest in such
places, but always in trees. The man, however, insisted that he had seen a large brown
eagle building a nest there, and he had also
seen one of the old birds diving for fish some

days before. He thought this was strange; for both the brown and bald eagle obtain their food by robbing the fish hawks after they have risen from the water with their prey in their beaks. The man told Audubon that he could soon satisfy himself, as the old birds would soon come to feed their young with fish, as he had seen them before.

Audubon placed himself a hundred yards from the foot of the cliff, and waited in impatient curiosity. In about two hours the old bird made his appearance, welcomed by the loud hissings of two young ones, which crawled to the extremity of a hole in the cliff to receive a fine fish. Audubon had a perfect view of the noble bird as he balanced himself on the edge of the rock, his tail spread and his wings partly open. In a few moments the female bird, a little larger, joined her mate, having also brought a fish. She was more cautious than her mate; she glanced her quick eye around, and instantly perceived that her abode had been discovered. She dropped the fish with a loud shriek, communicating the alarm to the male. They both hung over our heads, keeping up a growling cry, as if attempting to frighten us from our suspected design against

the nest. They picked up the fish which the
female had just dropped, and found it to be
a white perch, weighing five and a half
pounds. They made arrangements to return the next morning with guns and men,
to secure, if possible, both the young and
old birds. A storm hindered the expedition
until the third day, but when they reached
the rock they found that the sagacious birds,
suspecting such an attempt, had removed
their young to new quarters.

It was two years from this time, after
having made many fruitless excursions, that
he obtained the great desire of his heart.
About a mile from the village of Henderson,
while returning home, he saw an eagle rise
from a small inclosure not a hundred yards
before him. He had been feasting upon the
remains of some slaughtered hogs, and un-
willing to leave with his appetite yet unsatis-
fied, he lit upon the branch of a tree over-
hanging the road. Audubon carefully prepared his gun and walked slowly toward
the place. The eagle awaited his approach,
looking upon him with an undaunted eye.
He fired and the eagle fell. Words could
hardly express the exultation of Audubon
over his prize. He felt "a pride," he says,

" which they alone can feel who, like me, have devoted themselves from their earliest childhood to such pursuits, and who have derived from them their first pleasures."

"To those who may be curious to know my reasons," he adds, "for giving to the bird the name it bears, I can only say, that, as the new world gave me birth and liberty, the great man who insured its independence is next to my heart. He had a nobility of mind and a generosity of soul such as are seldom possessed. He was brave, so is the eagle; like it, too, he was the terror of his foes; and his fame, extending from pole to pole, resembles the majestic soarings of the mightiest of the feathered tribe. If America has reason to be proud of her Washington, so has she to be proud of her great eagle."

The male bird weighed fourteen and a half pounds; it was three feet seven inches in length, and the extent of its wings was *ten* feet and two inches.

The *white-headed eagle* is the bird best known under the general name of his species.

It is the bird that is borne on our national standard, " bearing," Audubon says, little thinking of the possibility of the civil war which is now staining the land with blood, "to distant lands the remembrance of a great people living in a state of peaceful freedom. May that peaceful freedom last forever!"

This eagle is noted for his wonderful strength, for his daring, and for his courage. He is a ferocious bird, and the terror of weaker birds and even small animals. He is the lion of the air. Audubon thus pictures a common spectacle, illustrating the character and habits of this powerful bird. It occurs on the Mississippi, late in the fall, when approaching winter brings millions of water-fowl from the north, seeking a milder climate for a few months. "The eagle is seen, perched in an erect attitude, on the highest summit of the tallest tree by the margin of the broad stream. His glistening but stern eye looks over the vast expanse. He listens attentively to every sound that comes to his quick ear from afar, glancing now and then on the earth beneath, lest even the light tread of the fawn may pass unheard. His mate is perched on the opposite side, and should all be tranquil and silent, warns him by a cry to continue patient. At this well-known call the male partly opens his broad wings, inclines his body a

little downward, and answers to her voice
in tones not unlike the laugh of a maniac.
The next moment he resumes his erect attitude, and again all around is silent. Ducks
of many species are seen passing with great
rapidity, and following the course of the
current ; but the eagle heeds them not ; they
are, at this time, beneath his attention. The
next moment, however, the wild, trumpet-
like sound of a yet distant but approaching
swan is heard. A shriek from the female
eagle comes across the stream, for she is as
fully on the alert as her mate. The latter
suddenly shakes the whole of his body, and
with a few touches of his bill, arranges his
plumage in an instant. The snow-white
swan is now in sight; her long neck is
stretched forward, her eye is on the watch,
vigilant as that of her enemy; her large
wings seem with difficulty to support the
weight of her body, although they flap in-
cessantly. The eagle has marked her for his
prey. As the swan is passing the dreaded
pair, the male bird, in full preparation for
the chase, starts from his perch with an awful scream, that, to the swan's ear, brings
more terror than the report of the large
duck gun Now is the moment to witness

The Eagle and its Prey.

No 720.

the display of the eagle's powers. He glides through the air like a falling star, and, like a flash of lightning, comes upon the timorous swan, which now, in agony and despair, seeks, by various maneuvers, to elude the grasp of his cruel talons. It mounts, doubles, and willingly would plunge into the stream, were it not prevented by the eagle, which, long possessed of the knowledge that by such a stratagem the prey might escape him, forces it to remain in the air by attempting to strike it with its talons from beneath. The hope of escape is soon given up by the swan. It has already become much weakened, and its strength fails at the sight of the courage and swiftness of its antagonist. Its last gasp is about to escape, when the ferocious eagle strikes with its talons the under side of the wing, and with unresisted power, forces the bird to fall in a slanting direction upon the nearest shore." Great is his exultation over his prey. He presses the dying swan under his powerful feet, driving his sharp claws into his heart. He shrieks with delight as he feels the last convulsions of his prey. The female has watched every movement of her mate. She now sails down to the spot where he eagerly awaits her, and when she arrives, they turn the breast of the luckless swan upward, and gorge themselves with gore.

At other times, when the eagles discover a wild goose, a duck, or a swan sailing along on the water, they accomplish their capture in a very shrewd way. Knowing that these water-fowl can dive at their approach, and thus escape them, they ascend into the air in opposite directions over the river or lake on which they have observed the object of their pursuit. After both eagles have reached a certain height, one of them immediately dashes with great swiftness at the bird upon the water. But the latter expecting, and prepared for this, dives the moment before the eagle reaches the spot. The pursuer then rises into the air, while his mate dashes down as the poor victim rises from the water to breathe. Down he dives again, as the eagle just glances him, and arises once more; but he hardly raises his head again for a another breath when down comes the other eagle like an arrow. This is kept up until the wearied victim, unable to continue his diving, stretches out its neck and swims for the shore, to hide among the rank weeds,

It is of no avail; the moment it approaches the margin, one of its pursuers darts upon it and kills it in an instant.

During the spring and summer it has even a much less honorable way of securing its living. As soon as the fish hawk makes its appearance from the South, following the lines of the great rivers, the eagle offers himself, an unbidden companion, to them. Perched on some tall summit in view of the water-courses, he watches every motion of the fish hawk while on the wing. When the latter rises with a fish in his grasp, the eagle rushes upon him, and snatches his hard-earned meal. As the fish hawk rises from the water, the eagle, glancing from his height, poises himself over him. The hawk, fearing for his own life, drops the fish. In an instant the eagle, carefully estimating the rapid descent of the fish, closes his wings, and with the swiftness of thought follows it, seizing it before it reaches the water.

The eagle, however, is not confined to such food, but greedily devours young pigs, lambs, fawns, poultry, and putrid carcasses of every description. It has been known even to attack and destroy young children.

The eagle is supposed to live to a very

great age—some persons have thought to
even a hundred years. Audubon once took
a female bird that he judged must have been
very aged. Its tail and wing-feathers were
so worn out and so rusty, that he imagined
the bird had lost its power of moulting or
shedding them. The legs and feet were covered with large warts; the claws and bill
were much blunted; it could scarcely fly
more than a hundred yards at a time, and
the body was poor and tough. The eye was
the only part which appeared to have sustained no injury. It remained sparkling and
full of animation, and even after death re-
tained its luster.

The white-headed eagle is seldom seen
alone; two of the different sexes having become acquainted, continue together until one
dies or is destroyed. The nest, which is of
great size, is usually placed on a very tall
tree, which is destitute of all its lower
branches. It is made of sticks from three to
five feet in length, large pieces of turf, rank
weeds, and Spanish moss when it can be
found. It measures, when finished, from
five to six feet in diameter, and so great is
the accumulation of materials that sometimes
it measures the same in depth; the same

nest being occupied for a great number of years, and additions being constantly made to it. It can, of course, be seen at a great distance. Commonly two or three eggs are laid; they are of a dull white, equally rounded at both ends. The young birds appear in about three weeks. The attachment of the parents to the young is very great when the latter are of a very small size. To ascend to the nest at this time would be dangerous. As they grow older, and are able to take wing, if they are not disposed to fly off, the old birds turn them out of the nest and beat them off. They are fed when in the nest with fish, rabbits, squirrels, young lambs, pigs, opossums, etc. The bird is four years of age before it attains the full beauty of its plumage. It is universally known in this country as the bald eagle. This is founded on the erroneous idea that its head is bare, but this is not the case; the head is densely covered with white feathers, which, contrasting with the dark tints of the body, give it the bald appearance which has determined its common name. When the eagle sleeps, he snores with a hissing sound so loudly as to be heard in the perfect silence of the night for a hundred yards; yet so light is his sleep that the cracking of a stick under the foot of a person immediately awakens him.

The shriek of the steam-whistle has driven them back from the Mississippi, where they formerly gathered in great numbers, although many linger around their old haunts. Audubon expresses his regret that this bird has been chosen as the representative of our country, agreeing with Dr. Franklin, who wrote: "For my part, I wish the bald eagle had not been chosen as the representative of our country. He is a bird of bad moral character; he does not get his living honestly; you may have seen him perched on some dead tree, where, too lazy to fish for himself, he watches the labor of the fishing hawk; and when that diligent bird has at length taken a fish, and is bearing it to his nest for the support of his mate and young ones, the bald eagle pursues him and takes it from him. With all this injustice he is never in good case; but, like those among men who live by sharping and robbing, he is generally poor, and often very lousy. Besides, he is a rank coward; the little king-bird, not bigger than a sparrow, attacks him boldly, and drives him out of the district. He is, therefore, by no means a proper emblem for the

brave and honest Cincinnati* of America, who have driven all the *king-birds* from our country; though exactly fit for that order of knights which the French call *Chevaliers d'Industrie.*†

BALTIMORE ORIOLE.

Audubon found his lonely voyages up the Mississippi, and along the then lonely banks of the Ohio, often beguiled by the rich melody and brilliant plumage of the Baltimore oriole. Beautifully and devoutly he says: "In solitudes like these the traveler might feel pleased with any sound, even the howl of the wolf, or the still more dismal bellow of the alligator. Then how delightful must it be to hear the melody resulting from thousands of musical voices that come from some neighboring tree, and which insensibly leads the mind, with whatever it may have previously been occupied, first to the contemplation of the wonders of nature, and then to that of the great Creator himself."

* Our revolutionary patriots; so called from the brave *Roman Cincinnatus*, who left his plow to save his country.

† Thieves and pickpockets.

In early autumn on these rivers, at that period, never for days would the traveler be without the company or song of the oriole. It comes from Mexico, and perhaps farther South, and enters Louisiana as soon as spring opens there. It searches among the trees around the planters' houses for a suitable place to pass the season. Having made choice of a twig on a suitable tree, the male bird commences his work. He flies to the ground, searching for the longest and driest threads of moss; and when he finds one fit for his purpose, ascends to the chosen spot, uttering all the while a continual chirrup, significant of his feeling of safety and content. No sooner does he reach the appropriated branch, than with bill and claws he fastens one end of the moss to the twig, with as much ingenuity as a sailor might do it. He then takes up the other end, which he secures also to another twig a few inches off, leaving the thread floating in the air like a swing, the curve of which is some seven or eight inches. The female comes to his assistance with another thread of moss or cotton, examines the work of her mate, and immediately commences operations for herself, placing her threads in a contrary direction; making the whole cross and recross, so as to form an irregular net-work.

Audubon says of them: "Their love increases daily, as they see the graceful fabric approaching perfection, until their conjugal affection and faith become as complete as in any species of birds with which I am acquainted."

The nest is thus woven from the bottom to the top, and secured so that no tempest can carry it off without first breaking the branch upon which it is fastened. If, instead of stopping in Louisiana, the birds had gone on to Pennsylvania and New York, as many of them do, they would then have lined their swinging nest with cotton or wool, and have taken special care to place the nest where the sun's rays would fall most powerfully upon it. But here in Louisiana, as if they knew that the heated term would soon be upon them, they take care to have the nest on the north-east side of the tree, where the winds can have full play, and it is lined throughout with the softest moss, but in such a way that the air can pass easily through it. From four to six little eggs are laid, about an inch in length, pale brown, dotted and spotted. In fourteen days the little charge makes its appearance. A day or two before the young leave the nest they creep in and out, clinging to its side, and thus strengthening their limbs. After leaving the nest they follow their parents for a fortnight, and are fed by them. After this they take care of themselves, feeding upon berries and insects. Their movements on the branches of trees will be noticed to differ from all others. They often cling by their feet, and stretch out their neck, body, and legs, in order to obtain an insect at a distance from them. They glide rapidly along the smallest twigs. Their motions are very elegant, and their song, which consists of from four to ten notes, is loud, full, and mellow, and extremely agreeable to the ear. When the season is over, and the weather becomes somewhat chilly, they start for a warmer climate; flying high over the trees in a straight line during the day, and alighting at night for food and sleep.

The plumage of the oriole is very beautiful. The general color is a brownish yellow, tinged with olive on the head and back. It is often kept in cages, feeding on figs, raisins, hard-boiled eggs, and insects. In the summer it is found in every state in the

Union; but it becomes partial to certain districts, so that of two places within twenty miles of each other, while not one is seen in the one, they will abound in the orchards and groves of the other.

MOCKING BIRD.

One of the most remarkable birds of our southern forests is the mocking bird. He imitates readily the song of every other bird of the grove, and all the numerous sounds of nature. No other bird in the world shares this wonderful power with him. These imitations are not with a harsh and unmelodious tone, like the parrot; but, with a mellowness that is indescribable, and a brilliancy of execution exceeding the original, it pours out one bird-song after another.

The mocking bird remains during the whole year in Louisiana. During the summer months many visit the north, as far, often, as Massachusetts. When those that have taken this journey come back, toward the last of October, they are instantly recognized by those that have remained at home, and are fiercely attacked.

The mocking birds begin to build their nests about the middle of April. Audubon gives a very lively account of the love-making between the male and female, as they introduce themselves to each other. The male flies around his mate, with motions as light as those of a butterfly. "His tail is widely expanded, he mounts in the air to a small distance, describes a circle, and again alighting, approaches his beloved one, his eyes gleaming with delight, for she has already promised to be his, and his only. His beautiful wings are gently raised, he bows to his love, and again bouncing upward, opens his bill and pours forth his melody, full of exultation at the conquest he has made." Having arranged his domestic relations, he pours forth his notes with more softness and richness than ever. He soars higher, dances through the air, full of animation and delight, imitating all the notes of the various songsters of the grove, rushing rapidly from one to another. For a while, each long day and pleasant night are thus spent; but at a peculiar note of the female, he ceases his song and attends to her wishes. A nest is now to be prepared, and the wisdom of both is required to settle this important question. The various fruit-trees are carefully examined, and as the bird seems to

know that it is a favorite of man and will
not be harmed, it ordinarily fixes its new
home quite near to the house, perhaps upon
the tree whose branches shade the window.
Dried twigs, leaves, grasses, cotton, flax, and
other substances, are picked up, and carried
to a forked branch, and there arranged.
When the female lays her first egg, the male
redoubles his attentions; and when the
whole number of five is completed, he seems
to have nothing else upon his hands but to
while away the hours, as his mate sets in the
nest, in tuning his pipe afresh and charming
her with his melody. Every now and then
he spies an insect upon the ground, the taste
of which he thinks will be relished by his
companion. Down he drops upon it, takes
it in his bill, beats it against the earth, and
flies to the nest to feed and receive the warm
thanks of his devoted mate. In a fortnight
the little birds demand the care of both parents. The dew-berries from the fields, or
the small fruits of the garden, mixed with
insects, supply food for the hungry little
brood. In a fortnight more the young birds
are flying from the nest, and leave their parents, as they are now able to take care of
themselves.

The mocking bird is fond of the sea-shore, and abounds there, seeking the low sands and low patches of bushes and briars. Nothing disturbs the female more than to have her eggs moved. She notices exactly how she leaves them, and if there has been a change she utters a low, mournful note, at the sound of which the male joins her, and they appear to condole together. After such an occurrence, she can hardly be induced to leave her nest until the eggs are hatched.

Different species of snakes ascend to their nests, to suck the eggs, or to swallow the young. On such attacks, not only the pair to which the nest belongs, but many other mocking birds from the vicinity, fly to the spot, rush upon the reptile, and in many cases are so fortunate as to force him to retreat, or even to deprive him of life. In the winter they approach the farm-houses, living about the gardens and out-buildings. They are often seen perched upon the house-tops and chimneys. When the weather is mild, the old males are heard singing with as much spirit as during the spring and summer.

The common cry or call of the mocking bird is a very mournful note. When migrating it travels by day, not taking long flights, but moving from tree to tree through the forests that skirt the great rivers. In its passage it keeps up this mournful call. Hawks sometimes attempt an attack upon the mocking bird; but the little creature defends itself with great courage, and by its cry summons all the birds of its species to its aid. These all raising the alarm, rush against the common foe and affright him from his purpose.

The birds are often placed in cages and sold for large sums of money. They can be easily raised by the hand when taken from the nest about ten days old. They often, when thus trained, become so familiar and affectionate as to follow a person about the house. Mr. Audubon knew of one raised from the nest, kept by a gentleman of Natchez, which would fly from the house and pour out its wild melodies in the open air, and then return at the sight of the keeper. It is, altogether, one of the most interesting birds of our groves.

PURPLE MARTIN.

One of the most familiar acquaintances of my readers among the birds is the purple martin. It reaches Massachusetts from its winter-quarters at the South about the twenty-fifth day of April, and they keep moving to the North as the summer opens. They commence their journey back about the twentieth of August. In coming north they assemble in immense flocks. Audubon saw one that extended, when in flight, about a mile and a half in length and a quarter of a mile in breadth. They move at a slow rate. Audubon walked easily under a flock for several miles, keeping up with them, his eye constantly upon them, watching their movements, much to the surprise of the persons who met him, engaged in their usual pursuits. It was by such careful observations that Audubon made himself so familiar with the habits of birds.

When the time comes for their return South they assemble in parties of from fifty to a hundred and fifty, about the spires of churches in the cities, or on the branches of large dead trees about farms. From these places they are seen constantly dashing off in a westerly direction for several hundred yards, uttering a peculiar cry, when, suddenly checking themselves in their flight, they sail back again to their starting-place. They seem in this way to be getting themselves into proper training, and to be ascertaining the right direction for the long journey before them. When they alight after such an excursion "they spend the greater part of their time in dressing and oiling their feathers, cleaning their skins, and clearing, as it were, every part of their dress and body from the insects which infest them." They remain exposed on their airy roosts at night, instead of resorting to the comfortable homes where they were reared in the tops of outbuildings. At length, on the dawn of a calm morning, they start with one accord, and are seen moving due west or south-west, joining other parties as they proceed, until the flock becomes as large as those that start from the South.

It is astonishing what a power of flight these little birds possess. When they meet a violent storm of wind, they appear to slide along the edge of it, as if determined not to lose an inch of what they have gained. The leaders front the storm without flinching, plunging through the blasts of the tempest, while the rest follow close behind, huddled together into such a compact mass as to appear from below as a simple black spot in the air. Not a twitter is then to be heard from them; but the instant they pass beyond the power of the blast they relax their speed to refresh themselves, and set up one united twitter, as if congratulating themselves upon the successful issue of their conflict with the storm.

The martin is very expert at bathing and drinking while on the wing. When over a large lake or river, they dart down, skimming the surface, and dipping beneath the wave with a rapid motion of the rear part of the body, then rising and shaking off the water like a spaniel. When intending to drink, they sail close over the water, with both wings gently raised, forming a sharp angle with each other. In this position they lower the head, dipping their bill several times in quick succession, and swallowing a little water each time. These little birds are very courageous and persevering, never yielding what they consider their rights. They very much dislike cats and dogs, and often, together, make an attack upon crows and hawks, and are frequently seen to follow and tease the eagle, whenever he approaches in sight of the martin's box.

Audubon had a large and comfortable house built and fixed upon a pole near his residence for the martins. One winter, after the martins had been in possession of their homestead two seasons, he put up several small boxes in order to induce the bluebirds to build their nests in them. In the spring the martins came on, and thinking these smaller apartments more comfortable than their own, drove out the beautiful bluebirds, and took forcible possession of them. The bluebirds were very reluctant to leave their nests, fighting with great bravery for them, but were overpowered by the heavier blows of their enemies. One bluebird, especially, hung around his nest and annoyed the martins as much as possible, while he would only show his head outside of the box, and pour out his impertinent exultations. Audubon concluded to aid the bluebird; so he caught the martin and clipped his tail with a pair of scissors, hoping that this mortifying punishment would induce him to remove to his own tenement. But no sooner was he launched into the air with his abbreviated tail than back he rushed to the box again. Audubon caught him again and clipped both wings, so that his flight was much affected; but still he held upon his stolen home, and it was only with his life that he could be driven away from it.

The twitter of the martin, although not melodious, is very pleasing. The bird is a universal favorite. Its hurried notes are the earliest sounds of tne morning, waking the laborer to his toils and cheering him in it.

The Indians are fond of the bird, putting up for it a calabash (the shell of a pumpkin, or like vegetable) on some projecting twig near their cabins. On this pleasant cradle the martin makes his res.dence, and drives the vultures and other birds of prey from the deer-skins and pieces of venison drying around the cabin. And Audubon says: "The humbled slave of the southern states takes much pains to accommodate this favorite bird. The calabash is neatly scooped out and attached to the bending top of a cane near his hut. It is, alas! to him a mere memento of the freedom which he once enjoyed; and at the sound of the horn which calls him to his labor, as he bids farewell to the martin, he cannot help thinking how happy he should be were he permitted to gambol and enjoy himself day after day with as much liberty as that bird." Noble sentiment, when we consider the period at which it was written. While we are recording it, it looks as if God had opened the door before the imprisoned slave, and, amid terrible scenes of bloodshed and distress arising out of a civil war in his behalf, had said to the poor slave, From this hour *thou shalt be free!*

Their nests are built about the twentieth of April, a few days after its arrival from the South; the material being dry sticks, willow-twigs, grasses, leaves green and dry, and whatever rags it can pick up. Many pairs resort to the same box, and live together, with their little broods, in perfect harmony. The eggs are pure white, and from four to six are laid. Two broods are raised in a season. The male bird is exceedingly attentive while the female is confined to the nest, flying frequently past the door, twittering upon the box, sometimes taking his turn upon the nest, and bringing food for the family. The food consists entirely of insects, so that their services to the farmer in destroying the foes to his fruits and vegetables are invaluable.

9

RUBY-THROATED HUMMING BIRD.

We have seen how carefully Audubon studied the habits of the largest birds that make their homes in our forests; with the same painstaking observation he turns his attention toward the smallest. It is not surprising that the charming little humming bird should awaken a deep interest in one so alive to every beautiful thing. "Where is the person," he says, "who, on seeing this lovely little creature moving on humming winglets through the air, suspended as if by magic on it, flitting from one flower to another, with motions as graceful as they are light and airy, pursuing its course over an extensive continent, and yielding new delights wherever it is seen—where is the person, I ask, who, on observing this glittering fragment of the rainbow, would not pause, admire, and instantly turn his mind with reverence toward the almighty Creator, the wonders of whose hand we at every step discover, and of whose sublime conceptions we everywhere observe the manifestations in his admirable system of creation?"

As soon as the flowers appear in the open-

ing summer this bright little sprite is on its
tireless wing, "carefully visiting every opening flower-cup ; and, like a curious florist,
removing from each the injurious insects that
otherwise would ere long cause their beauteous petals to droop and decay. Poised in
the air, it is observed peeping cautiously and
with sparkling eye into their innermost recesses; while the etherial motions of its pinions, so rapid and so light, appear to fan and
cool the flower, without injuring its fragile
texture, and produce a delightful murmuring
sound, well adapted for lulling the insects to
repose. Then is the moment for the humming bird to secure them. Its long, delicate
bill enters the cup of the flower, and the pro-
truded double-tubed tongue, delicately sensible, and imbued with a glutinous saliva,
touches each insect in succession, and draws
it from its lurking place, to be instantly
swallowed. All this is done in a moment,
and the bird, as it leaves the flower, sips so
small a portion of its liquid honey that the
theft, we may suppose, is looked upon with
a grateful feeling by the flower, which is thus
kindly relieved from the attacks of her de-
stroyers."

The little creature is always, when seen,

in such rapid motion that the wonderful beauty of its plumage can hardly be distinguished. The brilliancy of its throat is marvelous. Sometimes it glows with a fiery hue, and again it is changed to the deepest velvety black. The upper parts of its delicate body are of resplendent, changing green. It moves from one flower to another like a gleam of light, upward, downward, to the right, and to the left. It moves north as fast and as far as the warm summer weather admits, and hurries back to the tropical groves long before the frosts appear. Audubon says, with great tenderness and beauty, "I wish it were in my power at this moment to impart the pleasures which I have felt while watching the movements and viewing the manifestations of feelings displayed by a single pair of these most favorite little creatures when engaged in the demonstration of their love to each other: how the male swells his plumage and throat, and, dancing on the wing, whirls around the delicate female; how quickly he dives toward a flower, and returns with a loaded bill, which he offers to her to whom alone he feels desirous of being united; how full of ecstacy he seems to be when his caresses are kindly received; how his little wings fan her as they fan the flowers, and he transfers to her bill the insects and the honey which he has procured with a view to please her; how these attentions are received with apparent satisfaction; how, soon after, the blissful compact is sealed; how, then, the courage and care of the male are redoubled; how he even dares to give chase to the tyrant flycatcher, hurries the blue bird and the martin to their boxes; and how, on sounding pinions, he joyously returns to the side of his lovely mate. All these proofs of the sincerity, fidelity, and courage with which the male assures his mate of the care he will take of her while sitting on her nest, may be seen, and have been seen, but cannot be portrayed or described. Could you cast a momentary glance on the nest of the humming bird, and see, as I have seen, the newly hatched pair of young, little larger than humblebees, naked, blind, and so feeble as scarcely to be able to raise their little bill to receive food from the parents; and could you see those parents, full of anxiety and fear, passing and repassing within a few inches of your face, alighting on a twig not more than a yard from your body, waiting the result of your unwelcome visit in a state of the utmost despair, you cannot fail to be impressed with the deepest pangs which parental affection feels on the unexpected death of a cherished child. Then how pleasing it is, on your leaving the spot, to see the returning hope of the parents, when, after examining the nest, they find their nurslings untouched! These are the scenes best fitted to enable us to partake of sorrow and joy, and to determine every one who views them to make it his study to contribute to the happiness of others, and to refrain from wantonly or maliciously giving them pain."

This beautiful lesson these little birds taught Audubon; happy will it be for us if we also learn it.

Audubon could hardly satisfy himself whether the humming bird migrated by day or night, but thought it probable in the latter, as they seem to be always feeding during the day. It is almost impossible to follow their flight on account of the smallness of their size. A person standing in a garden near a common althea in bloom will be surprised suddenly to hear the humming of their wings, and then in an instant to see the birds themselves near him. In a moment again they rise into the air, and are out of sight and hearing almost instantly.

These little birds have a peculiarly delicate nest. Its outside is formed of the light gray moss found on branches of trees and old fence-rails. These are glued together by the saliva of the bird. They then line it with some cottony substance, and finally secure the silky fibers obtained from many plants, exceedingly soft and delicate, for the inner surface. On this soft bed two little pure white oval eggs are laid. In ten days the young birds appear. In one week they are ready to fly, but are fed still another week by their parents. The principal food of the humming bird is the insect which it finds in flowers, and the honey of the flower itself. They are somewhat quarrelsome, having frequent battles in the air. Should one be feeding on a flower and another approach it, they both immediately arise into the air, twittering and twisting in a spiral manner until out of sight. After having fought out their battle the victor returns to the flower.

We might, with great pleasure and profit, multiply these studies among the birds by Audubon; but our object has been simply to show how he passed the long hours of solitude when far from his home; how he occupied the time that he snatched away from business, to awaken, if possible, a desire in the minds of our readers to examine the large volumes which he published, recording in full the results of a long life of unwearied observations, on land and water, in every portion of our widely extended country; and finally, to arouse a personal love for nature in their breasts, impelling them forth into God's beautiful world to study for themselves his marvelous creations.

With so many interesting works upon natural history, it would not be a long work, certainly not a weary one, to become familiarly acquainted with every bird that visits our vicinities—its habits, its food, and its distinguishing songs. The study is becoming the more valuable, as the birds are found to be the best friends the farmer has in his fruit orchard and garden; and their retreat from our groves would prove the ruin of the trees by the various insects which now form in immense multitudes their food.

They teach also such gentle and beautiful lessons, and they so immediately speak of the wisdom, and goodness, and providence of their Creator, that no one can continue in such a study without feeling his heart deeply moved with a sense of the divine presence and the divine goodness.

CHAPTER VII.

AUDUBON'S EXPERIENCE IN PUBLISHING.

In April, 1824, Audubon visited Philadelphia, bringing some of his drawings with him. He had scarcely a friend in the city, excepting Dr. Mease, who had visited him in his younger days, and proved to be a friend indeed. The doctor introduced him to Charles Lucien Bonaparte, who was himself an interested and successful student of natural history, and had published four superbly illustrated volumes, intended rather as a continuation of the work of Wilson, whom he assisted in his labors. Prince Musignano, for that was his title, was much pleased with the drawings of Audubon, and introduced him to the Natural History Society of Philadelphia. This introduction to the prince, and the encouragement he received from him, proved the turning-point in the life of Audubon. He had sought out these beautiful histories of the birds simply for the pleasure it gave him; now he determined to make a complete survey of all the principal birds of our forests, to take full-size drawings of them, and become perfectly familiar with their habits. With the exception of the prince, he found but little sympathy in Philadelphia, and started for New York. He was warmly received here, and encouraged in his undertaking. His spirits, always sensitive to neglect, and somewhat depressed by his experience in Philadelphia, were elevated; and with good courage he ascended the Hudson and sailed across the lakes, seeking the wildest solitudes, to enter upon his self-denying labors. In these forests, he says, "for the first time I communed with myself as to the possible event of my visiting Europe. I began to fancy my work under the multiplying efforts of the graver. Happy days, and nights of pleasing dreams! I read over the catalogue of my collections, and thought how it might be possible for an unconnected and unaided individual like myself to accomplish the grand scheme." He divided his drawings into three different classes, depending upon the size of the objects they represented, and these formed the foundations of the first three volumes of his great work. "I improved the whole," he says, "as much as was in my power; and as I daily retired farther from the haunts of man, determined to leave nothing undone which my labor, my time, or my purse could accomplish."

During the execution of this mighty plan, a misfortune occurred to him that would have discouraged any man but one of an unconquerable will, and a childlike reliance upon Providence.

He had occasion to leave his home in Henderson, Ky., to visit Philadelphia on business. He placed all his drawings carefully in a wooden box, and gave them into the charge of a relative, with an injunction to see that no injury happened to them. He was absent several months, and when he returned one of his earliest inquiries was in reference to his treasure, as he called it. The box was brought forth and opened. "But, reader, feel for me," he says with affecting simplicity. "A pair of Norway rats had taken possession of the whole, and had reared a young family among the gnawed bits of paper, which but a few months before represented nearly a thousand inhabitants of the air!" Poor Audubon! the trial was terrible. None but a brave and trusting nature would have rallied under it. "The burning heat," he says, "which instantly rushed through my brain was too great to be endured without affecting the whole nervous system. I slept not for several nights, and the days passed like days of oblivion." Finally his strong nature rallied; he took his gun, his note-book, and his pencils, and went forth to the woods again as buoyantly as ever. He loved the work, and it was not simple toil to repeat his labors. A noble ambition seized him to make his drawings much better than before. Within a period of three years he had filled his portfolio again, and began now seriously to consider his plan for giving the world the result of his studies, and publishing such a work on the birds of America, both as to size and correctness of drawing, as had never before been seen. The engravers of Phila-delphia assured him that his drawings could never be engraved; and other difficulties rendering it impossible to publish them in New York, Audubon, not to be diverted from his purpose by ordinary difficulties, determined to visit England, and submit his pictures to the skill of European en-gravers.

He had removed his family to Louisiana; and in 1826, taking his portfolio, he sailed for Great Britain. Being entirely a stranger, his heart sank within him as he approached the English coast. There was not an individual in the country that he knew, although he bore with him commendatory notes from eminent men in his own country to persons of distinction here. But how would he, a simple backwoodsman, be received! Might he not find individuals here whose superior talents would throw his own entirely in the shade! With a childlike trust in the care of Providence, he landed at Liverpool. His heart nearly failed him as he walked alone the crowded streets, meeting during the first two days not one glance of sympathy. He would have betaken himself with his gun to the woods for company, but there were none near. The presentation, however, of his first letter procured him a large circle of invaluable friends. Gentlemen of wealth and education immediately recognized the merits of his remarkable sketches, and took him at once by the hand. At their suggestion his pictures were publicly exhibited in the galleries of the Royal Institution of that town. "A prophet is not without honor save in his own country." The attention and patronage that Philadelphia refused, Liverpool now lavished upon him. In Manchester the same hearty welcome was repeated; and in Edinburgh, Scotland, he was received by the first scientific and literary characters, in his own touching language, "as a brother." All the principal societies of the arts and sciences enrolled him as a member. It was in this city that he commenced the publication of his immense work, although he found it advisable afterward to transfer the work of engraving to London.

His numerous and generous friends all advised him to issue his work in the form of a large quarto, (the size of a large family Bible,) as this could be sold at a reasonable price, and he could easily secure subscribers enough to richly remunerate himself for all his years of toil, and place his family in comfortable circumstances. But money was the last object that Audubon had in view; and even the advancement of his family, in this respect, weighed but slightly upon his mind.

He had nurtured, during his solitary hours in the wilds of America, the daring ambition of publishing a work such as the world never saw before. He had great confidence that he should be carried through the mighty undertaking.

He finally determined to issue it upon the

largest *elephant folio,* enabling him to de-
lineate the largest birds, such as the bald-
headed eagle, of the full size of life. This
made it necessary to ask a very large price
for the work. A thousand dollars was the
price which he placed upon the four magnificent volumes, a sum which only rich in-
stitutions and wealthy individuals could
afford to bestow upon such an object. "The
extreme beauty, however, of this splendid
work extorted the applause of the wealthy
and eminent in station," and some one
hundred and seventy subscribers, during the
ten years before its publication was completed, were obtained in England, France,
and America. It is said that this large sum
did not met the expense of the work, but
that he exhausted in addition the remains of
his own small fortune.

It was not merely that the birds were of
the size of life, and admirably engraved and
colored, that gave this work its peculiar interest and value, but they are represented in
all their characteristic and graceful attitudes;
you seem not merely to see a picture, but
the birds themselves. Both sexes and different ages, the very trees, shrubs, and
grasses where they stood when drawn from

nature, their nests and eggs, all are represented so vividly that you almost expect to hear their song and see them spread their wings for flight.

"Those who have turned over the leaves of Audubon's large book," says one, in a short sketch of his life, " or better still, who remember to have seen the collected exhibition he once made in the Lyceum of this city, (New York,) will recall with grateful feeling the advantages of his method. They will remember how that vast and brilliant collection made it appear to the spectator as if he had been admitted at once to all sylvan secrets, or at least, that the gorgeous infinity of the bird-world had been revealed to him in some happy moment of nature's confidence. All the gay denizens of the air were there, some alone on swaying twigs of the birch or maple, or on bending ferns and spires of grass; others in pairs, tenderly feeding their young with gaudy or green insects, or in groups pursuing their prey or defending themselves from attack; while others, again, clove the thin air of the hills, or flitted darkly through secluded brakes. All were alive, all graceful, all joyous."*

* " Homes of American Authors."

10

During the publication of his first volume he visited France, and was introduced to the first scholars and foremost men of the learned circles, of Paris. He was warmly received by the great naturalist, Baron Cuvier, under whose hospitable roof he spent many evenings in the society of the learned from all countries. He formed the acquaintance of Louis Philippe, then Duke of Orleans, and afterward king of the French, through whose influence he obtained many patrons of his work. Baron Cuvier paid his undertaking the high commendation of saying "that it was the most magnificent monument that art had ever raised to nature."

He had previously visited London. After leaving Edinburgh, on his way to this city, in order to introduce himself and his enterprise to the public, he had exhibited his pictures, with some of the engravings, in several large towns. "I cannot say," he remarks, " that the employment was a pleasant one to me, but it was a means of acquiring fame, of which I was desirous of obtaining a portion; and knowing that, should I be successful, it would greatly increase the happiness of my wife and children, I waged war against my feelings, and welcomed all who, from love of science, from taste, or from generosity, manifested an interest in the American woodsman."

His fervent, simple piety seems to be an abiding and comforting guest in his heart. When he reached Liverpool again in his journey, he says: "I felt my heart expand within me, and I poured forth my thanks to my Maker for the many favors which I had in so short a period received."

With mingled emotions of hope and fear, he trode the streets of London for the first time. His letters of introduction soon brought around him the best and highest society of the metropolis, and opened before him the richest opportunities for the improvement of his mind, and for the enlargement of his list of subscribers for his drawings. Thus wonderfully had a good Providence opened his way before him, and his highest desires, nourished in the forests of America, were fully realized.

His first volume of engravings was not ready for delivery until the close of 1830.

In April, 1829, he sailed again for America, to perfect the drawings for his coming volumes, and to prepare the descriptive work, entitled "Ornithological Biography," which accompanied each volume of engravings.

"With what delight," he says, "did I mark the first wandering American bird that hovered over the waters, and how joyous were my feelings when I saw a pilot on our deck. Before visiting his family, from whom he had been long separated, such was his self-denial that he scoured the woods of the middle states first, and reached them in Lousiana in the end of November."

Accompanied by his wife, he now made arrangements to return to England, where he arrived in the spring of 1830. Upon his reaching London he received a diploma, certifying his election as a member of the Royal Society of Arts and Sciences.

"Such an honor," he says, "conferred on an American woodsman, could not but be highly gratifying to him. I took my seat in the hall, and had the pleasure of pressing the hand of the learned president with a warm feeling of esteem."

His first volume of engravings, and of biographies, as he styled them, was now in the hands of his subscribers, and his artist was busily at work upon the second. Leaving his family with the warm friends he had made in England, he left on the first of August, 1831, for another and very extensive tour over his native land, in order to enrich his collection, and become more familiar by personal observation, both in their winter and summer haunts, with the habits of the birds whose lives and adventures he was writing, and whose portraits from nature he was gratuitously taking. Few men have exhibited such noble perseverance against difficulties and discouragements. It was ten years from the time of the appearance of his first illustrations before his third volume was given to the public. He calculated himself that it would take sixteen years to finish the work. Not one of his friends seemed to have the least hope of his final success, and some advised him to abandon his plan, sell his drawings, and return to his country. When he delivered his first drawings to the engraver he had not a single subscriber. He listened with attention to all that his friends urged in reference to the difficulties before him, but never for a moment seriously thought of abandoning the cherished object of his hopes.

"My heart was nerved," he says, "and

my reliance on that Power on whom all must depend, brought bright anticipations of success." About the time his second volume was completed (in 1834) a nobleman called upon him with his family, and requested him to show them some of his original drawings. In the course of conversation, Audubon was asked how long it would be before the work was finished. When he answered "in eight years," the nobleman shrugged up his shoulders, and sighing, said, "I may not see it finished, but my children will, and you may please to add my name to your list of subscribers." The young people exhibited an expression of mingled joy and sorrow, and Audubon sought to dispel the cloud that appeared to hang over the father's mind. His solemnity of manner greatly impressed our woodsman, and for several days his words were in his mind.

"I often thought," he says, "that I might not see the work completed; but at length I exclaimed, 'my sons may.'"

When his third volume was completed, in allusion to this he wrote:

"My trust in Providence is augmented, and I cannot but hope that myself and my family together may be permitted to see the completion of my labors."

However long the task to which he had set himself, Audubon enters upon his work, at the commencement of each volume, with the same unquenched enthusiasm and the same devout piety. In commencing the "Biographies" of the birds engraved in his second volume, he says:

"Leaving to others the task of repeating the mass of fabulous stories accumulated through ages about the different species of birds, I now resume my attempts to arrange the materials which I have obtained during years of laborious but gratifying observation of the manners of the feathered inhabitants of our American woods and plains. I shall confine myself to particulars which I have been able to gather in the course of a life spent in studying the birds of my native land, where I have had abundant opportunities of contemplating their manners, and of admiring the manifestations of the glorious perfections of their omnipotent Creator."

He seemed distinctly to feel that God had called him to this work of revealing glories in his beloved native land " which had been hidden since the creation, or seen only by the naked Indian." "Let me resume," he says, "my descriptions, and proceed toward the completion of a task which, with reverence would I say it, seems to have been imposed upon me by Him who called me into existence."

CHAPTER VIII.

FROM FLORIDA TO LABRADOR.

In August of 1831, leaving his family with friends in England, he returned to his own country for a more thorough exploration of its forests and shores, both north and south. He secured the assistance of two expert naturalists; and having now acquired a national reputation by the first volume of the superb work upon which he was engaged, he readily obtained letters of protection and assistance from President Jackson and the heads of government at Washington. So warmly was he received and encouraged by the president, that he devoutly prays : "May He who gave me being, and inspired me with a desire to study his wondrous works, grant me the means of proving to my country the devotedness with which I strive to render myself not unworthy of her."

He started with his companions southward, and at Charleston formed one of his most valuable and lasting acquaintances; securing at once the warm affection and hearty co-operation of Rev. John Buchanan, a cultivated scholar in every department of science, but particularly familiar with zoology and botany. His introduction to Mr. Buchanan was characteristic. In order to lose no time, by the first glimpse of day, on the morning after their arrival in Charleston, they started on an expedition through the adjoining fields and woods. They returned home loaded with spoils and covered with mud, attracting much attention by their singular appearance. As they reached their boarding-house, they noticed a gentleman on horseback near the door.

"Are you Audubon?" he said, as the woodsman and his assistants approached. Upon being answered in the affirmative, he leaped from his saddle and shook Audubon cordially by the hand. He insisted upon his removing, with his companions, at once to his house. Suitable apartments were assigned to them; servants, carriages, horses, and dogs were placed at their command; friends were pointed out to them, who accompanied them to the most interesting places for prosecuting his work among the birds. A large number of peculiarly interesting land and water-birds were added to his collections.

Through his letters from the government he was received on board the revenue cutter Marion, and passed the winter on the coast and among the Keys of Florida. He had proposed at first to draw and describe only land-birds, but, in consequence of numerous requests from the patrons of the work, he was induced to extend his inquiries to the coasts as well as among the forests.

The difficulties in studying the habits of water-birds are very great. If one has proper enthusiasm he can hardly fail of obtaining any bird he wishes upon the land, as they simply flit from bush to bush, and seldom fly beyond your vision. But the water-bird sweeps afar over the wide ocean, hovers above the surges, or betakes itself for refuge to the inaccessible rocks on the shore. " On the smooth sea-beach you can see the active sand-piper; on the rugged promontory the dusky cormorant; under the dark shade of the cypress the ibis and heron; above you, in the still air, floats the pelican or the swan; while far over the angry billows scour the fulmar and the frigate bird. If you endeavor to approach these birds in their haunts, they betake themselves to flight, and speed to places where they are secure from intrusion."

Audubon says, however, that with all these difficulties he seldom experienced greater pleasure than when, on the Florida Keys, under a burning sun, after pushing his boat for miles over a soapy flat, wearing out a long day, tormented by insects, in order to procure a heron new to him, he finally succeeded in his efforts.

Audubon's enthusiasm was powerfully aroused by the new world upon which he was entering. The gorgeous flowers of Florida, the singular and beautiful plants, the luxuriant trees, and the balmy air caused, he says, "his heart to swell with uncontrollable delight."

The birds which he saw were almost all new to him, and their lovely forms seemed to be arrayed in more brilliant apparel than he had ever before observed. As they gamboled among the bushes, or glided over the green waters, he longed for a more intimate acquaintance with them.

Some of the most interesting pages of Audubon's volumes contain the descriptions of these birds: the heron, the cormorant, the pelican, the ibis, the curlew, the tern, the petrel, the gull in all their varieties, and many others. Of the cormorant family the double-crested is the most noted. It resorts every spring, to lay its eggs and raise its young, to the bleak crags on the coast of Labrador, after passing its winter in lower latitudes. In long lines, sometimes forming angles, it hovers close over the waters in its flight. Occasionally it sails along, in a beautiful manner, at a considerable height above the surface. In order to rise above the water, into which it sinks so as to be nearly covered when swimming, it runs, beating the waves as it goes for many yards, as if seeking to obtain headway before it mounts on the wing. It is fond of sunning itself with extended wings; and at these times its glossy and beautiful plumage is seen to great advantage.

The Florida cormorant constantly resides near this southern peninsula. It seldom ventures out far to sea, and is rarely found a great distance inland from the shore, but follows the windings of the coast, and seeks the quiet inlets and bays. This is the only one of its kind that alights upon trees. It forms its nest in the groves of the dark mangrove. When it migrates, its flight is more rapid than other species of the same bird, and instead of sailing along, it is constantly propelling itself by flapping its wings. In cloudy weather these birds soar in wide circles high in the air, frequently uttering a note not unlike that of the raven. Should the atmosphere suddenly become cold, they gather into groups of fifty or a hundred, as if calling a council; when, arranging themselves in an angle, with double lines, as if in marching order, they fly swiftly toward the south. In fair weather they betake themselves in flocks to some rocky island, or to some cluster of trees upon the shore, and spreading their wings, bask for hours in the sunshine. Their food consists principally of fishes, for which they dive with great expertness.

On these southern shores is found the home of the great blue heron, on the margins of streams and around inland pools. Here he stands with his graceful neck extended and his bright eye fixed upon the water. The moment the unfortunate fish passes in his swift course, the bill of the heron divides the waters like a flash of lightning, and the wriggling victim tells of his certain aim. He is very suspicious; the moment he sees a person approaching he spreads his wide wings and soars aloft. They are very selfish birds, always alone except in the breeding season. Each one chooses his feed-ing ground, and fights away every intruder. Their enormous appetites make them dread a division of their spoils. They are, how-ever, very attentive to each other when the nests are occupied with eggs and with their young. It is at this time that their plumage is in perfection. They seem to show much anxiety to appear well to each other. Their nests are found often on the tops of tall cy-press trees, but sometimes near and even on the ground. They take turns in sitting upon the eggs, and feed each other at such times. Their food consists of fish, frogs, and small birds. The heron sits so gracefully upon the water that Audubon styles it the "lady of the waters." With a graceful motion, and a light and measured tread, it trips along the beaches and over the barrens without leav-ing a trace in the sand; showing to perfec-tion the glowing tints of its hanging crest, and the beautifully blended plumage of its back and wings and graceful tail. Light, irregular, and swift in its flight, it moves along with its companions, in an undulating manner, in long lines widely separated.

The Gulf coast is the home of the pelicans.

Here is the monstrous brown pelican, hovering over the waters, diving for his prey, or slumbering amid the branches of the mangrove. Although very heavy, they possess great powers of flight; being able not only to remain many hours on the wing, but to rise very high in the air, and to perform the most graceful evolutions. In pleasant weather great flocks of them gather together, as if for social enjoyment. They rise in the air together to the height of about a mile, and course in circles about each other; then suddenly, and with wonderful velocity, they dart downward and settle upon the waters, where they ride like a dusky fleet among the billows. When the tide goes down, they retire to the shore and rest upon the sand. They draw their heads between their shoulders, raise one of their feet, place their bills upon their backs, and thus take their naps. Immediately on the return of the tide, of which they have an unerring instinct, they all start up, spread their great wings, and soar in search of their prey. By watching their movements a very safe opinion may be formed of the coming weather. If they are seen fishing in retired places, it is a sure sign of a coming storm. If, on the contrary, they venture far out to sea, it is a certain indication of fair weather.

Another species of this bird is called the frigate pelican. These powerful birds are very much like vultures in their habits. They are rapacious, ferocious, and slothful. They are great thieves, as indolent persons are apt to be. They rob each other's nests, in order to construct their own with as little trouble as possible. They devour the young of all weaker birds, as well as prey upon the fish. They are very skillful in obtaining materials for their nests, so that they have no excuse for their thievish propensities; as they fly swiftly along they snap off the twigs from the trees with their powerful bills. His flight being swifter than the gull, or tern, or hawk, the frigate pelican often darts down from on high and snatches the prey from their mouths, which they have just seized from the sea. But now he must contend with his own companions. Several of them, observing his good fortune, rush toward him and surround him. Dashing at him, they writhe around him in wide circles, each one striking him with his wings as he reaches him, and seeking to tear the fish from his bill. This bird commences his search for

11

food very early in the morning, before the
sweet singers of the groves have begun their
melodies. He steals out in the dusky light
from his roosting place and sails over the
deep, eagerly watching for the unfortunate
fish that may approach the surface, when
he dashes down like an arrow upon him.
When the hurricane sends forward its misty
clouds, the thunders begin to roll, the light-
nings to flash, and the billows angrily toss
themselves on high, then this bird floats out,
gallantly awaiting the approach of the tempest. If he finds himself unable to force his
passage against its fury, he keeps his ground
by balancing himself in the air.

For three successive springs, this species
increases in the beauty of its plumage; the
green, purple, and bronze tints acquiring
greater distinctions.

The white pelican, when its snowy plumage is unsoiled, is extremely beautiful, and
differs only in its color from the others of
the same species.

Among the most common and striking of
the Gulf birds is the ibis, distinguished by
its colors and habits into the scarlet, the
white, the brown, the glossy, and the wood
ibis. The latter frequents the banks of for-

ent pools, swamps, and the pine barrens. In desolate recesses, where the dark cypresses are overhung with mosses, forming a complete shade, this bird will be found in its solitary grandeur. It is a very beautiful bird in plumage, but its habits are those of the vulture and pelican. It is one of the pirates of the waters and the woods.

The flamingo is remarkable for the splendor of its apparel. It is entirely scarlet, with the exception of the bill, half of which, and the points of each wing, are black. One of the most singular birds is the oyster catcher. This species is always found among the sands, or rocky shores of streams and bays opening from the ocean. It never flies inland. It is seldom seen in large numbers together. It has a very long, slender, but powerful bill. Its plumage, which is best seen when it is on the wing, is very handsome. Its flight is swift and graceful, oftentimes accompanied with remarkable evolutions. When flying in a small group they will suddenly check their course, and wheeling, return floating, not low over the waters, but soaring high in the air. Then they will abruptly check their flight, form into ranks, presenting a broad front, and, as if alarmed, will dive toward the sands or the waves. Should they perceive any one watching them, and they are always on the alert, they send forth a shrill cry of alarm, and fly at once entirely out of sight.

Audubon found that he could observe their habits only with a telescope. When it supposes itself perfectly safe, it is often seen thrusting its long bill into the sand. It is in this way it obtains its food, searching for crabs and oysters. It forces its bill like a chisel between the shells of the oyster, and feasts upon the tenant within. Sometimes it will dash the shell against the sand until it is broken, and its contents exposed. It does not form any regular nest, but scratches the sand until a hollow is formed, in which it deposits its eggs. While the sun shines the bird does not sit upon the eggs; when, however, the eggs are laid upon the bare rock, as on the coast of Labrador, the bird broods in the same manner as other species.

The deputy collector of Indian Key, when the Marian (or the lady of the green mantle, as the smugglers, who make these dangerous keys their resort, called her) crossed the coral reef (which stretches along the shore like an immense wall built by giants, but is simply the work of minute insects) and entered this inlet, fitted Audubon out with a boat and a pilot, and he at once entered upon his interesting search. While the assistants were engaged in procuring shells, plants, and small birds, the pilot said to him:

"Come along; I'll show you something better worth your while."

The boat was urged by its crew at a high speed until we approached a point, when the oars were taken in, and we were desired to be ready for what was to come. As we advanced, the captain quietly sculling the boat, there was a profound silence maintained, until, suddenly coming almost in contact with a thick shrubbery of mangroves, we beheld right before us a multitude of pelicans. A discharge of guns at once followed. The dead, the dying, and wounded fell from the trees upon the water, while the rest rose screaming into the air. Having taken their spoils, the pilot ordered his crew to pull away again, and the boat soon reached the extremity of the coral ledge. The boat was laid close under some four hundred nests of cormorants. They fired immediately, and from the number that dropped, as if dead, into the water, it appeared as if they had destroyed the whole colony. The pilot only laughed at them. "A blank shot, gentlemen," said he. "You should have waited until I gave you the word." Sure enough, one after another of the birds peeped up curiously out of the water and soon took to the wing; only a few had been injured. Their nests, which had been made of dry twigs, resisted the shot. They should have waited until the birds rose from their nests.

"The next morning," Audubon says, "was delightful. The gentle sea-breeze glided over the flowery isle, the horizon was clear, and all was silent save the long breakers that washed over the distant reefs. As we were proceeding to some keys seldom visited by men, the sun rose from the bosom of the waters with a burst of glory that flashed on my soul the idea of that power which called into existence so magnificent an object. The surface of the waters shone in its tremulous smoothness, and the deep blue of the heavens was pure as the world that lies beyond them. The heron heavily flew toward the land, like the glutton retiring at daybreak, with well-lined paunch, from the house of some wealthy patron of good cheer. The night-heron and the owl, fearful of day, with hurried flight sought safety in the recesses of the deepest swamps; while the gulls and terns, ever cheerful, gamboled over the waters, exulting in the prospect of abundance. I also exulted in hope; my whole frame seemed to expand. How much of beauty and joy is lost to those who never view the rising sun!"

After a row of twenty miles they reached the southern cape of Florida. The flocks of birds that covered the beaches here, and hovered over their heads, were so immense that they almost doubted their eyes. The first volley they fired brought down sixty-five great godwits. "Rose-colored curlews stalked gracefully beneath the mangroves, purple herons rose at almost every step we took, and each cactus supported the nest of a white ibis. The air was darkened by the multitude of wings, while on the waters floated gallinules, and other interesting birds." It was a day of strange and powerful excitements, and many additions were made to his portfolio. On their return to the cutter they had an experience of one of the severe hurricanes so common and fatal in these southern seas. It was nearly sundown, when a black cloud suddenly obscured the light, and the sails of their little boat began to swell with the increasing breeze. One sail was hauled in and secured; the other was closely reefed. A low murmuring sound was heard, and occasionally sharp flashes of lightning glanced across the dark masses of moving clouds. A furious cloud seemed now rushing toward them like an eagle on outstretched wings. They were not more than a cable's length from the shore, when the pilot said to them, calmly but decidedly: "Sit perfectly quiet, gentlemen; the boat cannot upset, my word for that, if you will but sit still; here we have it!"

Those who have not witnessed such a tornado can form little idea of its terrific grandeur. "One would think that, not content with laying waste all on the land, it must needs sweep the waters of the shallows dry to quench its thirst. No respite for an instant does it afford to the objects within the reach of its furious current. Like the scythe of the destroying angel, it cuts everything by the roots, as it were, with the careless ease of the experienced mower. Each of its revolving sweeps collects a heap that might be likened to the full sheaf which the husbandman flings by nis side. On it goes with a wildness and fury that are indescribable; and when at last its frightful blasts have ceased, Nature, weeping and disconsolate, is left bereaved of her beauteous offspring. In some instances even a full century is required before, with all her powerful energies, she can repair her loss. The planter has not only lost his mansion, his crops, and his flocks, but he has to clear his lands anew, covered and entangled with the trunks and branches of trees. The bark overtaken by the storm is cast on the lee-shore, and if any are left to witness the fatal results they are the 'wreckers' alone, who, with inward delight, gaze upon the melancholy spectacle."

The instant the blast reached their boat it shivered like a leaf. They thought it had gone over, but the next moment it was high upon the shore. Audubon turned to gaze upon the sublime and awful sight. The waters were drifted into heaps like snow; the tough mangrove bushes hid their tops amid their roots, and the loud roaring of the waves blended with the howl of the tempest. The rain did not fall, but masses of water flew in a horizontal direction, and struck him with the force of a smart blow. They were providentially saved. The storm had passed away in half an hour.

THE PIRATE'S DEATH.

Audubon, whose gentle and engaging manners won for him the warm regards of all the officers of the cutter, gathered from them not only much information in reference to his favorite birds, but whiled away many hours in listening to their adventures upon the dangerous coast along which they sailed.

One calm moonlight night, as he was admiring the wonderful beauty of the clear heavens, the officer of the watch entered into conversation with him. Of humble birth, in his early days he had been engaged in the turtle fishery, and in hunting wild game. By his native energy he had secured an education, and gradually risen to his present station. Among his early adventures he related this as occurring in a recess in the shores of the Gulf of Mexico while he was upon a hunting expedition.

It was drawing toward night, and seeking a good place to pitch his slight tent

No. 726.

Audubon listening to the Captain of the Watch.

among the canes upon the shore, as he paddled his boat along he came to the mouth of
a little stream, and proceeded a short distance
up the current, in order that his boat might
be beyond the effects of any sudden storm
upon the Gulf. As he moved up the stream
he suddenly came upon a very beautiful boat.
But on reaching it, what was his horror to
find its sides marked with blood stains; and
looking within, to find two human bodies
covered with gore. He knew that either
pirates or hostile Indians had been engaged in
this frightful work, and he felt no little fear
lest they might be still lingering in the vicinity. While deliberating as to the course he
should take, he heard, in the distance, the
groans of a person apparently in great agony.
Putting aside all fears for his personal safety,
he hastened in the direction of the sufferer,
carrying his gun loaded, and ready to be
fired, in his hand. As he cautiously picked
his way through the canes, a hand was seen
waving in the air in the most supplicating
manner. In the next moment the head and
breast of a man, covered with blood, were
raised up, and a faint, husky voice asked
for mercy and help. A death-like silence
followed as he sank back upon the earth.

The hunter looked carefully around to see if there were any foes upon the watch; but all was still save the croakings of the frogs, and the evening song of the insects. He hurried back to the stream, and filling his cap with water, he returned to the dying man. He washed his face and breast, rubbed his temples with some spirits that he carried in a vial in his pocket, and noticed more closely the features of the fainting man. He must have been a powerful man, as his chest was immense; but his face was hard and forbidding. He groaned in the most appalling manner as his breath struggled through the mass of blood that seemed to fill his throat. He noticed that a large pistol was thrust into his bosom, and a naked cutlass lay near him on the grass, while a red silk handkerchief was bound around his forehead. His appearance at once disclosed the fact that he was a pirate.

As the hunter bathed his temples he revived, and exhibited some signs of recovering. It was now dark, and he spoke of making a fire; but, as if fearing to be left alone, or to be discovered by the light of the flames, the pirate besought him to desist. He gathered, however, some kindlings, and soon a blaze lit up the darkness of the scene. He sought to stanch the flowing of the blood from the pirate's wounds, and to bind up the deepest gashes. It was the most extraordinary hour of the hunter's life. He tried to talk with the dying man upon religious subjects, but found that he hardly believed in the existence of God.

"Friend," said the bleeding man to him, "for a friend you seem to be, I never studied the ways of Him of whom you talk. I am an outlaw, perhaps you will say a wretch; I have been for many years a pirate. The instructions of my parents were of no avail to me, for I have always believed that I was born to be a most cruel man. I now lie here, about to die in the weeds, because I long ago refused to listen to their many admonitions. Do not shudder when I tell you, these now useless hands murdered the mother whom they had embraced. I feel that I have deserved the pangs of the wretched death that hovers over me, and I am thankful that one of my kind will alone witness my last gaspings."

To his further efforts to induce the miserable man to pray, he said,

"It is all in vain, friend; I have no objection to die. I want no pardon from *any one.* Give me some water, and let me die alone."

He tried to induce him to make some reference to the scene in which he lost his life, and give some information of his companions; but his answer was,

"It is impossible; there will not be time; the beatings of my heart tell me so. My wounds are mortal, and I must die without what you call a confession."

He brought him another cap full of water, and poured it slowly into his lips. The moon, in its mild beauty, now rose in the east. He pointed it out to the dying pirate, and asked him if could not in it see the hand of God.

"Friend, I see what you are driving at," was his answer; "you, like the rest of our enemies, feel the desire of murdering us all. Well, be it so; to die is, after all, nothing more than a jest; and were it not for the pain, no one, in my opinion, need care a jot about it. But, as you really have befriended me, I will tell you all that is proper."

He bathed his temples again, and washed his lips with spirits, hoping his mind might take a right direction. This was the substance of what he gurgled out of his throat

in broken English, all the while chok-
ing with blood. He inquired how many
bodies were in the boat, and when told he
said,

"That's right; they are the bodies of the
scoundrels who followed me in that infernal
Yankee barge. Bold rascals they were; for
when they found the water too shallow for
their craft, they left it and waded after me.
All my companions had been shot, and to
lighten my own boat I flung them overboard.
As I lost time in this, my two pursuers
caught hold of my gunwale, (side of the
boat,) and struck me on my head and body
in such a manner that after I had disabled and
killed them both in the boat I was scarce able
to move. The other portion of the Yankee
crew carried off our schooner and one of our
boats, and perhaps ere now have hung all my
companions whom they did not kill at the
time.

"I have commanded my beautiful vessel
many years, captured many ships, and sent
many rascals to the devil. I always hated
the Yankees, and only regret that I have not
killed more of them. I sailed from Matan-
zas. I have often been in concert with others. I have money without counting, but it

is buried where it will never be found, and it would be useless to tell you of it."

This was all the confession of the dying pirate. In this spirit he rushed into the presence of a pure God, and of the victims of his murderous hand. His throat filled with blood, his voice failed, the cold hand of death was laid upon his brow; feebly and hurriedly he muttered, "I am a dying man, farewell."

The officer, as he turned to Audubon, concluded his sad recital, saying,

"Alas! it is painful to see death in any shape; in this it was horrible, for there was no hope. The rattling in his throat announced the moment of dissolution, and the body fell on my arms with a weight that was unsupportable. I laid him on the ground. A mass of dark blood poured from his mouth; then came a frightful groan, the last breathing of that foul spirit; and what now lay at my feet? a mangled mass of clay."

He buried him in the sand, and with joy at his own escape from a conflict with the pirates, he launched his canoe and paddled out of the stream with a feeling of mingled gloom and abhorrence.

Audubon examined every part of the coast,

and with his companions obtained an abundance of rich materials for his remaining volumes. The Marion having occasion to visit the Tortugas, Audubon embraced the opportunity of examining these remarkable islands. They form a group of five or six low, sandy, uninhabitable banks, about eighty miles from Key West. Between these islands are deep channels, very intricate, and only safe to those that are perfectly familiar with them. The great coral reef or wall lies about eight miles from these sandbanks, upon which many a vessel has been wrecked. The whole surface of the islands is covered with corals, sea-fans, and innumerable shell-fish. Turtles of different species resort here to lay their eggs, and clouds of sea-fowl flock here every spring for the same purpose. Cargoes of eggs are gathered here and carried to distant ports.

It was a few hours before sunset when the Marion dropped her anchor near one of these islands. Audubon thought the sight of a sunset in these southern latitudes was worth a voyage for the purpose.

"Look at the great red disc," he says, "increased to triple its ordinary dimensions! Now it has partially sunk beneath the dis-

12

tant line of waters, and with its still remaining half irradiates the whole heavens with a flood of golden light. A blaze of refulgent glory streams through the portals of the west, and the masses of vapor assume the appearance of mountains of molten gold. The night hawk is flapping his noiseless wings in the gentle breeze; the terns, safely landed, have settled on their nests; the frigate pelicans are seen wending their way to distant mangroves; and the brown gannet, in search of a resting-place, has perched on the yard of the vessel. Slowly advancing landward, their heads only above the water, are observed the heavily-laden turtles, anxious to deposit their eggs in the well-known sands. On the surface of the gently rippling stream I dimly see their broad forms as they toil along, while at intervals may be heard their hurried breathings, indicative of suspicion and fear.

The moon with her silvery light now illumines the scene, and the turtle having landed, slowly and laboriously drags her heavy body over the sand, her *flappers* being better adapted for motion in the water than on shore. Up the slope, however, she works her way, and see how industriously she re-

The Baltimore Oriole.

No. 738

moves the sand beneath her, casting it out
on either side. Layer after layer she deposits her eggs, arranging them in the most
careful manner, and, with her hind paddles,
brings the sand over them. The business is
accomplished, the spot is covered over, and,
with a joyful heart, the turtle swiftly retires
toward the shore, and launches into the
deep."

There are four different species of turtles;
the *green* turtle, which is preferred as an article of food ; the *hawk-billed* turtle, the shell
of which is so valuable an article of commerce ; the *loggerhead* turtle, and the *trunk*
turtle, which sometimes grows to an enormous size, and has a pouch like a pelican. Its
shell and flesh are so soft that the finger can
be pushed into them almost as easily as into
a lump of butter. On this account this species is seldom eaten except by the Indians.
The turtles spend the winter in deep waters,
but in the spring they approach the shores
to lay their eggs, selecting the wildest and
most secluded spots for this purpose. They
approach the shores usually on fine moonlight nights. When thirty or forty yards
from the beach, the turtle raises its head
above the water and carefully examines the

shore. If everything appears quiet she pours forth a loud hissing noise, apparently to frighten away any intruders that may be prowling about the shores. If she hears any noise, or perceives any danger, she sinks into the water and goes off to a considerable distance; but if everything is quiet she advances slowly to the beach, and crawls over it, with her head raised to the full stretch of her neck. When she finds a favorable place for her eggs she again gazes around in silence. Finding all well, she proceeds to dig her hole in the sand to the depth of from eighteen inches to two feet. The eggs, to the number of from one hundred and fifty to two hundred, are then dropped one by one, in layers, into their nest. And now the turtle scrapes the loose sand back over the eggs, and so levels and smooths the surface that few persons on seeing the spot would imagine that it had been disturbed. The eggs are hatched by the heat of the sand. The moment her work is finished she starts for the water. Turtle hunters seize the opportunity, when they are upon the land, to capture them. They sometimes weigh several hundred pounds. Audubon was offered one weighing seven hundred. The first thing to be done is to turn them over upon their backs, when they become perfectly helpless. The turtle hunter falls upon his knees, and placing his shoulder behind the fore *flapper* of his victim gradually raises her up, and with a jerk throws her over. When the turtle is of a very large size, as is often the case, handspikes have to be employed. The turtle's bite is very fierce, but it can turn its head only a short distance, and may easily be avoided. Many beasts of prey, as well as the human kind, follow their tracks to discover their nests and rob them of their eggs; but their great skill in covering the surface defends the majority of them from harm. The turtle is sometimes taken in immense nets, and sometimes harpooned, when sleeping upon the water, like a whale.

" When I was in the Floridas," says Audubon, " several turtle hunters assured me that any turtle taken from the depositing ground and carried on the deck of a vessel several hundred miles, would, if then let loose, certainly be met with at the same spot, either immediately after or in the following season. Should this prove true, and it certainly may, how much will be enhanced the belief of the student in the uniformity and solidity of nature's arrangements, when he finds that the turtle, like a migratory bird, returns to the same locality, with perhaps a delight similar to that experienced by the traveler, who, after visiting distant countries, once more returns to the bosom of his cherished family."

Having examined every part of the coast visited by the revenue cutter, he returned to Charleston loaded with the spoils of the sea and of the shore. He now turned his steps to the eastward as summer opened, (the winter having been passed in the Floridas,) anxious to keep pace with the birds during their migrations. His family again met him at Philadelphia, and proceeded with him to Boston. His sons had now reached an age to offer him valuable assistance in his labors and studies, and they seemed to inherit much of his enthusiasm in the study of natural history. His eldest son, Victor Gifford, left them at Boston to return to England, to superintend the publication of the great work; while the younger son, John Woodhouse, accompanied his father on his eastern trip.

THE MEADOW LARK.

On the rich grass-fields not far from the sandy sea-shores of New Jersey, he found this beautiful bird in the greatest numbers. He watched its first entrance into its favorite summer resorts in the opening spring. It is interesting to see how deep and fresh are Audubon's emotions of joy as he welcomes his charming little friends and their rapturous songs. He is in the fields before sunrise; "the industrious bee is yet asleep, as are the birds in bush and tree; the small wavelets break on the beach with a gentle murmur; the sky is so beautifully blue, that, on seeing it, one fancies himself near heaven; the limpid dew-drops hang on every leaf, bud, and blossom. Anxious to view nature at her best, I lie waiting in pleasure for the next moment; it has come; all is life and energy; the bee, the bird, the animal, all nature awakens into life, and every being seems moving in the light of the divine countenance. Fervently do I praise the God who has called me into existence, and devotedly do I pursue my avocations, carefully treading on the tender grass until I reach a seat by nature's own hand prepared, when I pause, survey, admire, and try to understand all, yes, *all* around me. Delightful days of my youth, when, full of strength, health, and gladness, I often enjoyed the bliss of contemplating the beauties of creation! They are gone, never to return; but memory fondly cherishes the thoughts which they called into being, and while life remains will their memory be pleasing."

A lark, which had arrived from the south the evening before, now arises from the grass, refreshed by his rest, and rushing into the air pours out his melodious notes, hoping to hear a response from his female companion. The females sometimes lag a little behind in the great northern flight. "The male," as Audubon follows him with his eye, "is still on the wing. His notes sound loud and clear, as he impatiently surveys the grassy plain beneath him. His beloved is not there. His heart almost fails him, and, disappointed, he rises toward the black walnut-tree. I now see him, not desponding, as you might suppose, but vexed and irritated. See how he spreads his tail, how often he raises his body, how he ejaculates his surprise, and loudly calls for her. Ah! there comes the dear creature; her timorous, tender notes announce her arrival. Her mate has felt the charm of her voice. His wings are spread, and, buoyant with gladness, he flies to meet, to welcome her, anticipating all the bliss prepared for him. Would that I could interpret to you, as I feel them, the many assurances of friendship, fidelity, and love that at this precious moment pass from the one to the other as they place their bills together and chatter their mutual loves. Alas! it were vain to attempt it. I have listened to the talk, it is true; I have witnessed all their happiness; but I cannot describe it. You, reader, must watch them, as I have done, if you wish to understand their language."

At the foot of some tall tuft of grass they now prepare a nest. A round hole is scooped out in the ground, and in it is arranged a quantity of grass, fibrous roots, and other materials, disposed in a circle so as to resemble an oven. The leaves and blades of grass around are then so matted together as to cover and conceal it. The old birds take turns in setting upon the four or five little speckled eggs that are in the nest, and are unremitting in their attention toward each other at this time, and afterward in the care

of their offspring.   While the female is upon
the nest, the male, besides procuring food,
sits near and cheers her with his finest songs.

BOSTON.

Audubon was deeply impressed with the
hearty and generous reception that he met
from the educated and wealthy men of Boston.   His list of subscribers was considerably
increased, and every means that the city
offered, or that could be found in private
collections, was at once placed at his dis-
posal.   "Ah, reader," says Audubon, "my
heart fails me when I think of the estimable
friends whose society afforded me so much
pleasure in that beautiful city, the Athens of
our western world.   Never, I fear, shall I
have it in my power to return a tithe of the
hospitality which was there shown toward
us, or of the benevolence and generosity
which we experienced, and which evidently
came from the heart, without the slightest
mixture of ostentation.   Indeed, I must acknowledge that although I have been happy
in forming many valuable friendships in various parts of the world, all dearly cherished
by me, the outpouring of kindness which I

experienced at Boston far exceeded all that I have ever met with."

While Audubon was visiting Boston, Mr. Greenwood, proprietor of the museum, sold him a fine specimen of the golden eagle. Audubon was overjoyed at his magnificent purchase. "The eagle," he says, "was immediately conveyed to my residence, covered with a blanket, to save him, in his adversity, from the gaze of the people. I placed the cage so as to afford me a good view of the captive, and I must acknowledge that as I watched his looks of proud disdain, I did not feel toward him so generously as I ought to have done. At times I was half inclined to restore to him his freedom, that he might return to his native mountains; nay, I several times thought how pleasant it would be to see him spread out his broad wings, and sail away toward the rocks of his wild haunts; but then some one seemed to whisper that I ought to take his portrait, and I abandoned the more generous design of setting him at liberty for the express purpose of showing my friends his appearance. I occupied myself a whole day in watching his movements; on the next I came to a determination as to the position in which I might best represent him; and on the third thought of how I could take away his life with the least pain to him. I consulted several persons, and among others my most worthy and generous friend, Dr. George Parkman, who kindly visited my family every day. He spoke of suffocating him by means of burning charcoal, or killing him by electricity; and we finally concluded that the first method would probably be the easiest for ourselves and the least painful to him. Accordingly the bird was removed in his cage into a very small room, and closely covered with blankets; a pan of lighted charcoal was introduced, the windows and doors fastened, and the blankets tucked in beneath the cage. I waited, expecting every moment to hear him fall down from his perch; but after listening for *hours* I opened the door, raised the blankets, and peeped under them amid a mass of suffocating fumes. There stood the eagle on his perch, with his bright, unflinching eye turned toward me, and as lively and vigorous as ever! Instantly reclosing every aperture, I resumed my station at the door, and toward midnight, not having heard the least noise, I again took a peep at my victim. He was still uninjured, although the air of the

No. 726.

The Golden Eagle

closet was insupportable to my son and myself, and that of the adjoining apartment began to feel unpleasant. I persevered, however, for ten hours in all, when, finding that the charcoal fumes would not produce the desired effect, I retired to rest wearied and disappointed. Early next morning I tried the charcoal anew, adding to it a quantity of sulphur; but we were nearly driven from our house in a few hours by the stifling vapors, while the noble bird continued to stand erect and look defiance at us whenever we approached his post of martyrdom. His fierce demeanor precluded all internal application, and at last I was compelled to resort to a method always used as a last expedient, and a most effectual one. I thrust a long pointed piece of steel through his heart, when my proud prisoner instantly fell dead, without even ruffling a feather.

"I sat up nearly the whole of another night to outline him, and worked so constantly at the drawing that it nearly cost me my life. I was suddenly seized with a spasmodic affection that much alarmed my family, and completely prostrated me for some days."

The golden eagle frequents the upper waters of the Hudson and the lake countries. Audubon saw it afterward hovering over the dreary crags of Labrador.

It does not, like the white-headed eagle, seize its prey when on the wing; but the keenness of its vision enables it to mark its prize at a great distance, and driving through the air with the swiftness almost of lightning, it fastens upon the helpless victim. Audubon says its motions as it soars high in the air are most majestic, and worthy of this monarch among birds. The nest of this eagle is placed invariably upon some high and rugged cliff, and can be approached only at great risk to the invader. In the war of the Revolution a company of soldiers, stationed near the highlands of the Hudson, discovered a golden eagle's nest in a cleft of the rocks, midway between the summit and the river. One of the soldiers was let down by his companions, suspended by a rope fastened round his body. On reaching the nest he found himself suddenly attacked by the eagle. In self-defense he drew the only weapon he had, his knife, and made repeated passes at the bird. When, to his horror, he accidentally struck the rope that held him and nearly severed it. It began to unravel. The men

above, seeing the danger, instantly but carefully drew him up, relieving him from his peril-
ous position, he constantly expecting every
instant to be dashed to the gulf below. So
powerful was the effect of the terror upon
the soldier, that before the lapse of three
days his hair became quite gray.

About the middle of August, with companions obtained in Boston, he rambled over
Maine and the adjoining British provinces.
They made excursions into all parts of the
country, ransacking the woods and shores,
and finding constantly new friends proffer-
ing him their willing aid, and new accessions
to his knowledge of his feathered companions. He found valuable assistance from the
lumberers, who spend the winters in cutting
the immense pines that form the vast forests
of Maine, and floating them down the great
rivers to the towns and cities, where they
are sawn into lumber and exported to a
thousand different ports. In the summer, as
the smaller streams become shallow, many of
these logs are lodged, and ingenious plans
are resorted to in order to float them down
to the mills.

A TIMBER DRIVE.

In the month of September, in the town of Dennisville, in Maine, Audubon witnessed such an operation. The creek that conveyed the logs to the mill-pond was interrupted in its course by many rapids and narrow gorges with high banks. One of these gorges was about a mile above the mill-dam, and it was so rocky and rugged as to render it impossible to float the large logs through it at low water. Thousands of logs had accumulated in it. They lay piled in confused heaps to a great height along an extent of several hundred yards, in some places so close together as to form a kind of dam. Above the narrow gorge there was a large natural reservoir, where the waters seemed to gather and spread out into the appearance of a pond. Across the gorge the lumberers raised a temporary barrier with the refuse boards from the saw-mill. The boards were planted upright, and fastened at their tops to a strong tree, extending across the creek. These boards were secured at the bottom by braces, which could be easily removed. The dam was soon

completed, so that very little water escaped
through it. In two or three weeks the
water rose to the top of the high dam.
Early one morning he was summoned to see
the result of the experiment. Two lumberers, throwing off their jackets, tying
handkerchiefs around their heads, and fastening a long rope to their bodies, the end of
which was held by three or four others, who
stood ready if necessary to drag their companions ashore, were prepared for their peril-
ous adventure. Each one now taking an
ax, walked along to the braces in the center of the dam, and at a given signal knocked
them away, leaping with great dexterity
themselves from log to log to the shore,
almost with the quickness of thought.
Scarcely had they reached it when the
waters burst forth with a horrible roar.
All eyes were now bent toward the huge
heap of logs in the gorge. "The tumultuous burst of the waters instantly swept
away every object that opposed their progress, and rushed in foaming waves among
the timbers that everywhere blocked up the
passage. Presently a slow, heavy motion
was perceived in the mass of logs; one might
have imagined that some mighty monster

18

lay convulsively writhing beneath them,
struggling with a fearful energy to extri-
cate himself from the crushing weight. As
the waters rose this movement increased,
the mass of timber extended in all directions, appearing to become more and more
entangled each moment. Now the rushing
water filled the gorge to the brim. The
logs once under way, rolled, reared, tossed,
and tumbled amid the foam as they were
carried along. Many of the smaller trees
broke across, from others great splinters
were sent up, and all were in some degree
seamed and scarred. Then in tumultuous
majesty swept along the mingled wreck, the
current being now increased to such a pitch
that the logs as they were dashed against
the rocky shores resounded like the report
of distant artillery, or the angry rumblings
of the thunder. It seemed to me as if I
witnessed the rout of a vast army, surprised,
overwhelmed, and overthrown. The roar
of the cannon, the groans of the dying, and
the shouts of the avengers, were thundering
through my brain, and amid the frightful
confusion of the scene there came over my
spirit a melancholy feeling, which had
not entirely vanished at the end of many

days." In a few hours nearly all the timber that had lain heaped in the rocky gorge was floating in the great pond of the millers.

All down the large rivers of Maine, during the spring and summer, the merry lumber men in their red shirts are still engaged in floating, or "driving" down, as it is called, the immense pines cut during the winter to the mills and harbors near the mouths of the streams. Many such wild and dangerous adventures as this recorded by Audubon mark the history of every season.

One principal object of his visit to Maine was to become acquainted with the " spotted or Canada grouse," called also "the spruce partridge." In the village of Dennisville, eighteen miles from Eastport, he became acquainted with the family of Judge Lincoln. Each of the sons seemed to have his own peculiar taste, and Audubon became soon strongly attached to Thomas, who from his youth had manifested a decided fondness for the study of birds and their habits. He was a perfect woodsman and marksman, and together they scoured the forests, and secured all the varieties they could reach of their feathered inhabitants. The breeding grounds of the grouse are the larch or hackmetack woods. They are very difficult to traverse. The whole ground is covered with a beautiful carpeting of velvet moss, over which the light-footed partridges walk or run with ease, but Audubon and his companion would sink at every step nearly to the waist. In such places, difficult of access, these birds usually remain. They make their nests beneath the low horizontal branches of the fir-trees, carefully concealed. It is made of twigs, dried leaves, and mosses, and here from eight to fourteen eggs of a deep fawn color are laid. Only one brood is raised in a season, and they follow the mother like chickens as soon as hatched. All the species of this bird indicate the approach of rainy weather or a snow-storm far more accurately than the best barometer. On the afternoon previous to such weather they all resort to their roosting places several hours earlier than they usually do. Audubon noticed that flocks of them often went to roost at midday, or as soon as the weather felt heavy, and he found that it generally rained before night. When the flock remained busy in search for food until sunset, he found the night and day following clear.

THE BURNING FOREST.

Audubon's piety seems to have been a simple, constant, filial reliance upon the heavenly Father, ever and powerfully awakened by every object in nature that specially exhibited the wisdom and love of God, and always expressing itself in devout thanks for daily mercies, and in a hearty sympathy with the devotions of others.

"How delightful to me it has been," he says, "when kindly received under a friendly roof by persons whose means were as scanty as their generosity was great, I have entered into conversation with them respecting subjects of interest to me and received gratifying information. When the humble but plentiful repast was ended the mother would take from the shelf the Book of books, and mildly request the attention of her family while the father read aloud a chapter. Then to heaven would ascend their humble prayers, and a good-night would be bidden to all friends far and near. How comfortably have I laid my weary frame on the buffalo hide, and covered me with the furry skin of some huge bear."

Such a night he passed during one of his excursions in Maine, and as the next day was very rainy, he accepted the invitation of his hosts to remain with them. The spinning-wheel in the hands of the daughter commenced its merry music, and the boys busied themselves with their school books, while the father and his visitor sat in interesting conversation together. Allusion having been made to great fires in the woods by the mother, Audubon asked him to what she referred.

"A number of years before," he said, "terrible fires had occurred in the woods around them; she and I, and all of us, have good reason to dread them."

Audubon had read of them at the time, but desired to have an account of them from the lips of one who witnessed them.

At the time they occurred all the larch or hackmetack trees were nearly killed by in- sects cutting their leaves, which is fatal to evergreens. After destroying the larch, they attacked the spruces and pines with the same blasting results. These insects were in form like the caterpillar, about three quarters of an inch in length, and as green as the trees upon which they fed. These dead trees, well seasoned, afford ready fuel for a fire. Many thought the Indians set the woods on fire, but Audubon's host thought they might have occurred by the accidental fall of one large tree upon another: rubbing together fire would be started, and being covered with pitch, the wind would soon fan it to a blaze. While they were talking a rush of wind down the chimney blew the blaze of fire out into the room. The wife and daughter started involuntarily for the door, imagining for the moment that the woods were again on fire. Returning when they understood the cause, the lumberer continued his conversation.

"Poor things!" said he. "I dare say that what I have told you brings sad recollections to the minds of my wife and oldest daughter, who, with myself, had to fly from our home at the time of the great fires."

At the request of Audubon he related the circumstances. They were sound asleep one night, in a cabin about a hundred miles from their present residence, when, about two hours before daylight, they were suddenly awakened by the snorting of the horses and the lowing of the cattle. The lumberer caught up his rifle and rushed to the door, when he was struck by the glare of light reflected on all the trees before him, as far as he could see through the woods. His horses were leaping about, snorting loudly, and the cattle ran wildly among them with their tails straight over their backs. On going back of the house he could hear plainly the crackling made by the burning brush-wood, and saw the flames in an extended line approaching the house. He ran to the house and hurried up his wife and child. He could only take with him the little amount of money he had, and managed, for-tunately, to catch two of his best horses. Taking his child in one arm, he mounted one horse, and his wife the other. As they start-ed he looked back once more, and saw that the frightful blaze had already reached the rear of the house. His hunting-horn hap-pened, fortunately, to be fastened to his clothes, and he blew it, to collect, if possible, his dogs and cattle around him. The cattle followed for a while, but before an hour had elapsed they all ran as if mad through the woods, and that was the last he saw of them. The dogs, that were usually perfectly obedient,

now rushed on after the flocks of deer that
went bounding by them, as if fully aware
that death was upon her track. They heard
the blasts of the horns of their neighbors in
different directions, urging their way from
the devouring flames. He thought of a
large lake some miles off, which might pos-
sibly check the flames; and urging his wife
to whip up her horse, they set off at full
speed over the fallen trees and heaps of
brush.

They soon began sensibly to feel the heat,
and they feared that their horses would drop
every instant. A singular kind of breeze
passed over their heads, and the glare of the
atmosphere shone brighter than the daylight. His wife looked pale, and he was
sensible himself of faintness. The child's face
was flushed with the heat. Ten miles were
soon bounded over by the fleet horses.
When, however, they reached the lake, covered with sweat and quite exhausted, their
hearts sank within them. The heat of the
smoke was insufferable, and sheets of blazing
fire flew over them. They coasted the side
of the lake opposite the wind, and finally
gave up their horses, which they never saw
again. They went down into the rushes by

the edge of the water and laid themselves down flat, as their only chance of escaping the flames. The waters cooled and refreshed them. On went the fire, rushing and crashing through the woods; the whole heavens were in a perfect glare. Their bodies were cool enough, but their heads were scorching. The little girl, now apprehending the danger, almost broke their hearts with her cries.

The day passed on, and they became hungry from their long fast. Wild beasts plunged into the water, and came and stood near them, as if seeking their protection. Faint and weary, he managed to shoot a porcupine, and they all tasted its flesh. The terrible night finally passed away. The ground was covered with smoldering fires, and the trees stood like pillars of flame. The stifling and sickening smoke still rushed over them, and the burnt cinders and ashes fell thickly about them. He could hardly tell how they got through the night, for some of the time he was unconscious. Toward morning, although the heat did not abate, the smoke became less, and puffs of fresh air came occasionally to them. They began now to shiver with the cold, having remained so long in the water. They went to a burning log and warmed themselves; but what was to become of them they could not think. His wife hugged her child to her breast and wept bitterly; "but God," said the lumberer, "had preserved us through the worst of the danger, and the flames had gone past, so I thought it would be ungrateful to him, and unmanly to despair now." Hunger began to press them, but deer were near them; and with his gun he soon secured one, and roasted its flesh upon the abundant coals. By this time the blaze of the fire had passed out of sight, but it was still dangerous to go among the burning trees. After a while they commenced their sad march. Taking his little girl, he led the way over the hot ground and rocks. After two weary days and nights, during which they suffered terribly, they reached the "hard woods," which had been free from fire. Soon after they came to a house, where they were kindly received.

"Since then," said the grateful woodsman, "I have worked hard and constantly as a lumberer; but, thanks be to God! here we are safe, sound, and happy."

BAY OF FUNDY.

Audubon, in the revenue cutter Swiftsure, enjoyed a very interesting and profitable cruise in the Bay of Fundy. On White Head Island, near the Island of Grand Manan, he found almost every tree of a wood covering several acres bearing nests of a certain species of gulls whose habits he was anxious to study. "What a treat," he says, "was it to find birds of this kind lodged on fir-trees, and sitting comfortably on their eggs! Their loud cackling notes led us to their place of resort, and ere long we had satisfactorily observed their habits, and collected as many of themselves and their eggs as we considered sufficient." A morning in the bay, when the air was filled with the melodious concerts of birds, awakened the liveliest interest in the mind of Audubon. As the day broke, "how delightful it was to see fair Nature open her graceful eyelids, and present herself, arrayed in all that was richest and purest, before her Creator. Ah, reader, how indelibly are such moments engraved on my soul! With what ardor have I gazed around me, full of the desire of being enabled to comprehend all that I saw! How often have I longed to converse with the feathered inhabitants of the forest, all of which seemed then intent on offering up their thanks to the object of my own admiration! The delightful trills of the winter wren rolled through the underwood; the red squirrel smacked time with his chops; the loud notes of the robin sounded clearly from the tops of the trees; the rosy grosbeak nipped the tender blossoms of the maples; and high overhead the loons passed in pairs, rapidly wending their way toward far distant shores. Would that I could have followed in their wake!"

Point Lepreaux Harbor, where they anchored, was noted for an Indian custom which interested Audubon. Several species of ducks that in myriads cover the waters of the bay are at times destroyed here in a very singular manner. When July has come, all the water-birds that are no longer capable of breeding remain, "like so many forlorn bachelors and old maids, to renew their plumage along the shores." At this period, when the birds are utterly unfit for flight, troops of Indians make their appearance in light bark-canoes, paddled by the squaws and papooses, (women and children.) They form their boats into an extended curve, and drive the birds before them with a terrific noise; shouting, and beating the water with their paddles. Terrified by the noise, the birds push rapidly through the water before them, seeking to escape. The tide is high, and every cove around the shore is filled with the ducks. The Indians cease to shout, and silently close up upon the helpless multitudes, and wait until the tide goes down, when each one seizing a stick, they rush upon their prey. In this way sometimes more than five hundred wild fowls have been destroyed.

Our readers have heard of the remarkable tides in the Bay of Fundy. Audubon could hardly believe the statements in reference to them until he witnessed their occurrence.

When the tide went down, the bed of the bay where they observed it was bare for nine miles, like a sandy wilderness; and when the tide began to flow in, it rose three feet in ten minutes, and at high water it was sixty-five feet deep above the sands that were bare a few hours before.

From the Bay of Fundy they proceeded to the coast of Labrador. A heavy mist covered the surface of the waters as they approached the harbor of Bras d'Or; and although it was daylight, they could not distinguish the coast of Labrador, then only a mile distant. An old fisherman from Eastport, who saw their signal, came out in his boat and piloted them through the narrow channel, guarded by two dangerous rocks, into the port. Here they were assailed by the powerful odor of the decaying and cured fish. A hundred fishing barks lay at anchor. Every deck was heaped with the fish, which brings annually so many vessels from different ports and nations to this stormy and rugged coast. Some of the crews were plying their nets in search of small fishes for bait; while others were strewing the salted cod over the naked rocks, under the drying rays of the sun. Stacks of fish, nearly cured, stretched along in close array to an immense distance.

When the mists were lifted from the scene a sublime prospect presented itself—high craggy cliffs, with masses of snow still hanging to their sides at the close of July, with cataracts rushing from under the ice furiously down toward the plain. As they gazed upon the novel scene the song of the shore-lark began to fill the air. "Man the whale-boat," cried Audubon to his young companions, "let us be off to the shore;" and soon they were all at the place where they had seen a lark alight. Never before had he enjoyed the rich song of this bird so fully, or succeeded in finding its nest; but here he found this charming singer in the full perfection of its plumage and song, and here he had an opportunity of studying its habits. The shore-lark breeds on the high and desolate tracts of Labrador, in the vicinity of the sea. The shore is one uneven surface of dark granite, covered with mosses and lichens, scattered about in large patches or tufts. Upon these the lark makes her nest. The moss is often so nearly the color of the bird that you can hardly discover her until your foot is almost upon the nest. As you approach too near for her comfort she flutters away, feigning lameness so cunningly that none but one accustomed to the sight can help pursuing her as a wounded bird. Her mate immediately joins her in this mimic wretchedness, uttering at the same time a note so soft and plaintive, that it requires a strong motive even to force a naturalist to disturb the poor birds in their little treasure

of eggs or young birds. The nest is scooped
out of the moss, and lined first with fine
grasses, and then with the softest feathers.
Four or five pale blue eggs, with brown
spots, make their appearance in the beginning of July. The little birds leave the
nest before they can fly, running about upon
the moss in company with their parents.
They run so nimbly that it is quite difficult
to take them. When thus pursued the old
birds follow directly overhead, pouring out
the most melancholy notes. "In several
instances," Audubon says, "they followed
us almost to our boat, alighting occasionally
on a projecting crag before us, and entreating
us, as it were, to restore their offspring."

The birds leave their northern homes for
the South about the beginning of September.
They start then at the dawn of day, and fly
without much order, in straggling bands, just
above the water. The birds spend their
winters in Massachusetts, in the vicinity of
the sea-shore and wide, sandy plains. They
seldom are found south of Maryland.

After they had been three weeks in the
country, one morning just at sunrise they
entered one of the small valleys between the
craggy cliffs. The beautiful verdure, the

14

numerous flowers that were sprinkled over the ground, the half-smothered pipings of the frogs, and the multitude of musquitoes, made the spot seem to Audubon, in this bleak land, one of peculiar liveliness. But his ear was even more delighted than his eye. He heard a note of surpassing power and sweetness coming from a species of the finch that he had never seen before, and seeming to be a compound between that of the canary and the European wood-lark. He shouted to his companions, and they all followed the charming songster as he flitted from bush to bush. Whenever he alighted he would commence afresh his song. The shot of Mr. Lincoln, one of his young friends, brought the bird down, and Audubon gave to it the name of the Lincoln finch. Its habits were found to resemble those of the song-sparrow. Like it, mounted on the topmost twig of the tallest shrub or tree it can find, it chants for hours.

THE EGGERS.

The eggers of Labrador is the appellation given to certain persons who devote themselves exclusively to plundering the nests of the wild birds on this uninhabited coast, with a view of selling them in distant ports. Audubon witnessed their cruel and improvident proceedings with horror. In a miserable craft, dirty beyond description, unpainted, unwashed, and sending forth a deadly odor, they creep along the coast, hiding under the shadow of the terrible cliffs, that seemed to have been arranged on purpose to provide an undisturbed resort for the myriads of birds that annually visit this desolate region of the earth for the purpose of rearing their young. The crew of this despicable vessel, eight in number, in their appearance correspond with their vessel.

In the middle of the afternoon they launch their boat and enter it, each with a rusty gun. At their approach clouds of birds rise screaming from the rocks, wheeling in circles in every direction. Thousands, however, still remain, standing over their eggs to guard them. The reports of muskets are heard, and dead or wounded birds fall upon the rock or into the water. Instantly the whole company of birds take flight, and the robbers commence their shocking work. They trample hundreds of eggs under their feet, crushing the half-formed chick within its shell, and bear off as many as they can load upon themselves, with the dead birds that they have shot. Thus they go from cliff to cliff, collecting all the fresh eggs and destroying the others. Audubon could not endure the sight.

"At every step," he says, "each ruffian picks up an egg, so beautiful that any man with a feeling heart would pause to consider the motive which could induce him to carry it off. But nothing of this sort occurs to the egger, who gathers and gathers until he has swept the rock bare. The dollars alone chink in his sordid mind, and he assiduously plies the trade which no man would ply who had talents and industry to procure subsistence by honorable means."

They are a drunken set of men, in constant and bloody quarrels with each other, and with other crews engaged in the same business. They gather all the eider down they can find, and massacre the birds in great numbers for their feathers. So constant are their depredations, that some species of birds that were very abundant formerly had abandoned their breeding-places and removed farther to the North, in search of a secure retreat. Such a war of extermination could not last long. The British government passed strict laws against these merciless robbers, and punished all that were caught selling their eggs in any of the provinces.

THE FRENCHMEN OF LABRADOR.

As the schooner lay at anchor in a beautiful basin on the coast, surrounded by high, rugged cliffs covered with a stunted verdure, while watching for birds one morning Audubon saw on the high rocks of a small island, separated by a narrow channel from the mainland, a dark object. Turning his telescope in that direction he saw a man on his knees, with clasped hands, and with his face inclined downward. Before him was a small monument of unhewn stones, supporting a wooden cross. Such an incident in that desolate land was as surprising as it was affecting. His curiosity was so much excited that, taking his boat, he soon landed upon the rock, and scrambled up to the place where the man still remained upon his knees. When his devotions were ended he rose and bowed to Audubon, speaking in very poor French. Audubon asked him why he had chosen such a dreary spot for his prayers.

"Because," said he, "the sea lies before me, and from it I receive my spring and summer sustenance. When winter approaches I pray fronting the mountains upon the main; for at this period the karaboos come toward the shore, and I kill them and feed on their flesh, and form my bedding of their skins."

Audubon was so struck with his singular appearance, and the peculiar character of his religious services, that he followed him to his hut to learn more about him. It was very low, formed of stones plastered with mud, the roof being thatched with weeds and moss. It was warmed by a large Dutch stove; a hole in the side, stuffed with rags, took the place of a window; the bed was a pile of deer skins; a bowl, a jug, and three old rusty muskets, with ammunition, formed his furniture. Eight Esquimaux dogs yelled and leaped about the visitor. It was too filthy a place to be visited long. The host was very polite; insisted on his taking some refreshment, and rushed out somewhere with a bowl, as if to obtain it. Audubon seized the moment to go into the air and catch a

No 726

Audubon and the Frenchman who lost his "Rum."

pure breath. It was June, and he was surprised to see how rapidly in this northern
latitude verdure had come forward. The
grasses had nearly reached maturity, and
flies and musquitoes filled the air, as if he
had been in a Florida swamp. The Frenchman returned looking very chop-fallen. Tears
ran down his cheeks while he told Audubon
that his barrel of rum had been stolen by
some prowling fishermen. He said he had
been in the habit of hiding it in the bushes,
to prevent its being carried away by these
merciless thieves; but he thought they must
have watched him in his constant walks in
that direction. "And now," said he, "I
can expect none until next spring, and God
knows what will become of me in the winter." One would suppose he might have
been in greater distress for food than for his
annual barrel of rum. He had resided here
for upward of ter. years, having run away
from the fishing vessel that brought him from
France. He expected to become rich some
day by the sale of furs, seal skins, eider-
down, and other articles which he collected
on these desolate shores, and sold to the
traders that made their regular visits to
Labrador. He told Audubon that, "except-

ing the loss of his rum, he had never experienced any other cause of sorrow, and that he felt as happy as a lord."

Proceeding along the rugged shores of the bay, Audubon fell upon another singular resident upon this inhospitable coast. Several small vessels belonging to him were lying in a small bay, or near a wharf jutting out into the water. A number of neat-looking houses enlivened the view. He met Audubon and his company at the landing—a gentleman in his appearance, and dressed in the style of his visitors. He expressed much pleasure at the announcement of Audubon's name, and to his astonishment said:

"My dear sir, I have been expecting you these three weeks, having read *in the papers* of your intention to visit Labrador."

They followed him to his comfortable mansion, and he introduced them to his wife and six robust children. The lady was a native of the country, but of French extraction, lady-like in her appearance, and sufficiently accomplished. The host, after a handsome repast had been furnished, offered them newspapers from different parts of the world, and showed them a small but choice collection of books. He pointed out to them his garden, where a few vegetables struggled to obtain sun and soil enough to ripen themselves. Looking upon the desolate country around, Audubon asked him how one who had received a liberal education, and had mixed in society, could thus seclude himself from the world.

"The country around," he said, "is all my own, much farther than you can see. No fees, no lawyers, no taxes are *here*. I do pretty much as I choose. My means are ample through my own industry. The vessels that come here for seal-skins, seal-oil, and salmon, give me in return all the necessaries and, indeed, all the comforts of life. What else could the world afford me?"

He seemed entirely to overlook the truth that we are placed in this world not simply to live through our allotted time, and to secure as much comfort as possible, but to labor for others; to make others comfortable, and to glorify our Maker and Redeemer. With all its relief from the perplexities of social life, this is a very low order of enjoyment and existence, but a step above animal life.

Audubon asked him about the education of his children. "My wife and I teach

them," he said, "all that it is *useful* for
them to know; is not that enough? My
girls will marry their countrymen, my sons
the daughters of my neighbors; and I hope
all of them will live and die in the country."
He had more than forty Esquimaux dogs,
who take in this country the place and perform the labor of horses. As they left, he
sent his regards to his brother-in-law at
Bras-d'Or, between one and two hundred
miles down the coast, and desired to have
them tell him that he would call upon him
when he visited his father-in-law. His wife's
father resided alone, some seventy miles below them. The journey, however, over these
long distances was rapidly made in winter
over the frozen snows, drawn by a pack of
dogs.

Audubon called upon the brother-in-law,
and had rather an amusing experience with
his kind but uncultivated wife. Their house,
which they had imported from Quebec,
fronted the Strait of Belle Isle, and over-
looked the coast of Newfoundland. The
house was not finished, but they were received cordially; and the lady, who had
once visited Quebec, seemed desirous of im-
pressing her guests with a lively idea of her

attainments. Learning that Audubon knew something of the fine arts, she pointed to several miserable blotches of prints that hung upon the bare walls and said they were *elegant* Italian pictures, which she had purchased of an Italian, who came there with a trunk full of them. The guests managed to keep their countenances. One true trait of an amiable character the good woman exhibited. One of her children had caught a little bird and was tormenting it. She quietly rose from her seat, took the little fluttering thing from the child, and kissing it, launched it into the air. This was certainly prettier than her *Italian* pictures. After offering them some excellent milk in clean glasses, the lady asked Audubon if he was fond of music, and if he ever played upon an instrument. He modestly remarked that he had a slight acquaintance with music. The lady remarked that it was her *forte;* that she was immoderately fond of music. She had sent her instrument, she said, to Europe to be repaired, but it would return that season, and then her children and herself would again perform many beautiful airs. She remarked that any one could use this instrument with ease, for when the children felt fatigued the servant played upon it for them. Somewhat surprised at the remarkable qualities of the instrument, and at the peculiar musical abilities of the family, Audubon asked her what kind of an instrument it was. She readily described it, as follows:

"Gentlemen, my instrument is large, longer than broad, and stands on four legs, like a table. At one end is a crooked handle, by turning which round either fast or slow, I do assure you we make most excellent music."

Audubon saw that the lips of his young friends opened, and their features began to draw down into a broad grin; but a look from him induced them instantly to recover themselves.

"It is a hand-organ that you have," said Audubon.

"Ah, that is it," she said laughingly, "it is a hand-organ, but I had forgot the name, and for the life of me could not recollect it."

The husband had seen much of the world, although he was not an educated man like his brother-in-law. He caught seals without number, lived comfortably, visited his father-in-law and the scholar by the aid of his dogs, of which he kept a great pack, bartered and sold the spoils of his hunting, and cared for nothing else in the world. He had the only horse that was to be found in that part of the country, and several cows. He had a reputation among his neighbors for kindness, every one speaking well of him. Every day that Audubon's company remained in the vicinity this uncultivated artist, but good mother and wife, sent them fresh milk and butter, refusing all compensation in return.

After passing the summer on the coast of Labrador, he sailed again for Boston, touching at Newfoundland, exploring its woods and rivers, and adding to his collections. They passed some time also in Nova Scotia, moving on with the birds as they returned from their northern homes.

To make still further observations, that nothing might be lacking to render his work full and accurate, he now moved on rapidly again to the South, where he passed another winter in completing his examinations, aided, as heretofore, by his generous and learned friend Bachman, of Charleston. In addition to the study of the birds and the painting of their plumage, he now carefully collected prepared specimens of all the birds described in his volumes.

In the following March (1834) he returned to New York, and with his family once more embarked on the packet ship North America for England. In this year his second volume of drawings and of biographies were completed and placed in the hands of his subscribers, and with the large and valuable collections that he had made during his long journeys and voyages on his native continent he entered at once upon the preparation of the third. This volume, after the most painstaking care, he was able to send from the press in 1837.

CHAPTER IX.

AUDUBON'S CLOSING LABORS.

HAVING placed his wife, now an invalid, in the care of the kindest friends in London, he made arrangements for another long tour of observation in his native land, in company with his eldest son. His plan, which he was not able fully to carry out, was to cross the continent, " gaze on the majestic wilds of the Rocky Mountains, wander along the green valleys of the Oregon, and search the shores of the Pacific Ocean and a portion of North Carolina." On the first of August, 1836, he embarked again for the United States.

Several others had now entered into the interesting fields which he had been for so many years cultivating. Audubon was a man of the most generous and sincere feelings, beyond envy and jealousy, and devoid of a false pride which would restrain him from availing himself of the valuable services of others.

Thomas Nuttall, Esq., of Salem, had crossed

the Rocky Mountains, prosecuting his studies in the various branches of natural history, and had brought back many new and rare birds, and made valuable observations upon their habits. These were kindly placed by Mr. N. at the disposition of Audubon, who most heartily availed himself of these treasures, and gave the most generous acknowledgments. Dr. Townsend, of Philadelphia, who was then absent on the Pacific coast, had a valuable collection, which his friends in that city, very reluctantly, allowed him to examine, through a mistaken and ungenerous fear that it might detract somewhat from the honor of Dr. T.

With several friends, and with every facility that the government of the United States could afford in the use of its revenue cutters, Audubon commenced another thorough examination of the Gulf shores, the mouths of the Mississippi, and the coast of Texas. On his return to Charleston, South Carolina, his oldest son was married to a daughter of Rev. Dr. Bachman, thus drawing closer the cords that had long bound these two devoted lovers of nature together. His second son afterward married another daughter of Dr. Bachman.

Having been absent about a year, he returned again to London, to be once more united with his affectionate family.

In 1837 he had the satisfaction of seeing his third volume in the hands of his subscribers, and the fourth and last advancing. In 1839 this labor of his life was completed. The number of the birds crowded into his last volume was so large that he found it necessary to publish two volumes of biographies to accompany it; so that, while there are four volumes of engravings, there are five volumes of biographies.

Audubon was now nearly sixty. One might suppose at the conclusion of such a mighty task his enthusiasm would have been somewhat abated, and he would have felt like seeking repose in the bosom of a happy family during the remaining years of his life. But he says at this time, "The adventures and vicissitudes which have fallen to my lot, instead of tending to diminish the fervid enthusiasm of my nature, have imparted a toughness to my bodily constitution, naturally strong, and to my mind, naturally buoyant, an elasticity such as to assure me that, though somewhat old and considerably denuded in the frontal region, I could yet perform on

15

foot a journey of any length, were I sure
that I should thereby add materially to our
knowledge of the ever-interesting creatures
which have for so long a time occupied my
thoughts by day and filled my dreams with
pleasant images. Nay, reader, had I a new
lease of life presented to me, I should choose
for it the very occupations in which I have
been engaged. The life which I have led
nas been, in some respects, a singular one.
Think of a person intent on such pursuits as
mine have been, aroused at early dawn from
his rude couch on the alder-fringed brook of
some northern valley, or in the midst of some
unexplored forest of the West, or perhaps on
the soft and warm sands of the Florida shores,
and listening to the pleasing melodies of
songsters innumerable, saluting the magnificent orb from whose radiant influence the
creatures of many worlds receive life and
light. Refreshed and invigorated by health-
ful rest, he starts upon his feet, offers his
prayers, gathers up his store of curiosities,
buckles on his knapsack, shoulders his trusty
firelock, says a kind word to his faithful dog,
and recommences his pursuit of zoological
knowledge. Now the morning is spent, and
a squirrel or a trout afford him a repast.

Should the day be warm, he reposes for a time under the shade of some tree. The woodland choristers again burst forth into song, and he starts anew to wander wherever the objects of his search may lead him. When the evening approaches, and the birds are seen betaking themselves to their retreats, he looks for some place of safety, erects his shed of green boughs, kindles his fire, prepares his meal, and as the widgeon, or blue-winged teal, or perhaps the breast of a turkey or a steak of venison sends its delicious perfumes abroad, he enters into his parchment-bound journal the remarkable incidents and facts that have occurred in the course of the day. Darkness has now drawn her curtain over the scene, his repast is finished, and, kneeling on the earth, he raises his soul to heaven, grateful for the protection that has been granted to him and the sense of the Divine Presence in this solitary place. Then wishing a cordial good-night to all the dear friends at home, the AMERICAN WOODSMAN wraps himself up in his blanket, and closing his eyes, soon falls into that comfortable sleep which never fails him on such occasions."

One hardly knows which to admire the

most, the wonderful drawings from nature which fill the four magnificent volumes, or the most entertaining and truthful description of the habits and characteristics of the birds, intermingled with his personal adventures, found in the biographies. Passing so often from one portion of the country to the other, his handsome and vigorous form, his pleasing manner, and his sharp, expressive eye became very familiar, as it was always welcome, wherever he moved. Sometimes where he was not known amusing mistakes occurred. His dress, when upon his hunting excursions, was provided with reference ·to durability rather than to beauty, and he often looked quite like a backwoodsman or a French *voyageur*. Once, when he had been scouring the northern forests and the lake shores, he came to the English village on the Canada side of Niagara Falls. He went to the large hotel and began to make himself at home, and avail himself of the many expensive conveniences of the place. The hotel keeper looked upon him with amazement. He thought, in his dirty, torn habiliments, that he must be some vagrant hunter or wandering boatman who did not apprehend the expense to which he laid himself liable in this fashionable hotel, and if he did was not in a condition to meet it. He was on the point of turning him out, when the soiled woodsman went to the register and wrote his name, Audubon. Even then, he had his suspicions lest he might be an impostor. But one of the guests of the house recognizing the famous naturalist in his strange garb, welcomed him in the warmest manner. The master of the hotel, not a little chagrined by his unfortunate mistake, sought to redeem his false step by making his attentions almost a burden to his guest.

Some travelers* upon a canal route in Pennsylvania (for railroads were not then in use) heard above the bustle of the crowd rushing on board at the hour of starting the familiar name of Audubon spoken. "Mr. Audubon is the last on the list," said the speaker; "I fear he will not get a bed, we are so crowded."

"What, is it possible Mr. Audubon can be on board?" they rejoined almost simultaneously. "He is the man of all others that we most wish to see. Where? Which is he?"

"He is actually in this very cabin," said their informant; "there," he added, point-

* Incident noticed in North American Review.

ing to a huge pile of blankets and fur, which, stretched upon one of the benches, looked like the substantial bale of some western trader.

" What, *that* Mr. Audubon!" exclaimed the travelers, whose names were at the moment called out by the captain as entitled to the first choice of berths. This privilege they openly renounced in favor of Audubon. And now the green bale stirred a little, half turned upon its narrow resting-place, after a while sat erect, and showed that there was a man inside of it! A patriarchal beard fell, white and wavy, down his breast, a pair of hawk-like eyes gleamed sharply out from the frizzy shroud of cap and collar. The lookers on drew near with a thrill of irrepressible curiosity. The moment their eyes beheld the outline of that noble face they felt that it could be *he*, and no one else. Audubon it was in this wilderness garb, hale and alert with sixty winters on his shoulders, like one of his old eagles, feathered to the heel.

The travelers, soon on intimate terms with their admired companion, were delighted in listening to the ever fresh relation of his exploits, discoveries, and experiences, peculiarly instructive on account of the immense stores of knowledge which he had collected, and from the accuracy of his information. When ashore, the travelers found he outstripped in walking, with perfect ease, his considerably younger companions; while the clearness and power of his vision showed how entirely the vigor of his constitution had been preserved. One clear, fine morning, when passing through a particularly picturesque region, his keen eyes, with an abstracted, intense expression peculiar to them, were gazing over the scenery, when suddenly he pointed with his finger to the fence of a field about two hundred yards off and exclaimed: "See, yonder is a fox-squirrel running along the top rail; it is not often I have seen one in Pennsylvania." As not one other person in the group who looked in that direction with him could detect the creature at all, his companions felt some doubt as to whether he could discern the object so distinctly as to discover its species. They curiously asked him if he was *sure* that it was a *fox-squirrel*. Audubon smiled as he answered, "Ah! I have an eagle's eyes."

Having completed his undertaking, Audubon, with his family, parting with sincere regret from the many esteemed and generous friends he had made in England and Scotland, returned finally to his native shores.

He purchased a country seat upon the banks of the beautiful Hudson river, a few miles above the city of New York, which bore the name of Minnieland. Here, embowered among oaks and elms, he built himself a comfortable residence, and settled his family, for so long a period without an abiding home. Some years after his return, one of the contributors to that interesting volume, published some years since, "The Homes of American Authors," thus describes a visit to his residence:

"A short walk through the forest from the river soon brought a secluded country house into view, simple and unpretending in its architecture, and beautifully embowered amid the trees. Several graceful fawns and a noble elk were standing in the shade of the trees, apparently unconscious of the presence of a few dogs, and not caring for the numerous turkeys, geese, and other domestic animals that gobbled and screamed around them. Nor did my own approach startle the wild beautiful creatures, that seemed docile as any of their tame companions.

"'Is the master at home?' I asked of a

pretty maid-servant who answered my tap at the door, and who, after informing me that he was, led me into a room on the left side of the broad hall. It was not, how-ever, a parlor, or an ordinary reception room that I entered, but evidently a room for work. In one corner stood a painter's easel, with a half-finished sketch of a beaver on the paper; in the other lay the skin of an American panther. The antlers of elks hung upon the walls; stuffed birds of every de-scription of gay plumage ornamented the mantle-piece, and exquisite drawings of field-mice, orioles, and woodpeckers were scat-tered promiscuously in other parts of the room, across one end of which a long rude table was stretched to hold artist materials, scraps of drawing paper, and immense folio volumes, filled with delicious paintings of birds taken from their native haunts.

"'This,' said I to myself, 'is the studio of the naturalist;' but hardly had the thought escaped me when the master himself made his appearance. He was a tall thin man, with a high arched and serene forehead, and a bright, penetrating gray eye. His white locks fell in clusters upon his shoul-ders, but were the only signs of age, for his form was erect, and his step as light as that of a deer. The expression of his face was sharp, but noble and commanding; and there was something in it, partly derived from the aquiline nose, and partly from the shutting of the mouth, which made you think of the imperial eagle.

"His greeting, as he entered, was at once frank and cordial, and showed you the sincere and true man. 'How kind it is,' he said, with a slight French accent, and in a pensive tone, 'to come to see me; and how wise too to leave that crazy city.' He then shook me warmly by the hand. 'Do you know,' he continued, 'how I wonder that men can consent to swelter and fret their lives away amid those hot bricks and pestilent vapors, when the woods and fields are all so near? It would kill me soon to be confined in such a prison house; and when I am forced to make an occasional visit there it fills me with loathing and sadness. Ah! how often, when I have been abroad upon the mountains, has my heart risen in grateful praise to God that it was not my destiny to waste and pine among those noisome congregations of the city.'

"Audubon was over sixty years of age

when the writer of this sketch made his acquaintance, and he was then as ardent in the prosecution of his studies, as bold in his projects for additional acquisitions, and as animated in his conversation and manner as he could have been forty years before. Indeed, he was, even at that advanced period of his life, on the eve of an excursion to the Rocky Mountains, in search of some specimens of wild animals of which he had heard; and the following year he passed the summer on the Upper Missouri and the Yellow Stone rivers. His love of his vocation, after innumerable trials, successes, and disappointments, was to the end of his life most intense."

Audubon's first important undertaking after his return to the United States was the republication, in a smaller and a cheaper form, of his great work upon the birds of our country. This edition he completed, and published in seven octavo volumes, the last being issued in 1844. It was to add to these volumes some new species of birds of which he had heard that he took the journey referred to above, to the headwaters of the Mississippi. Twenty additional species of birds were thus added to the Ameri-

can edition. This undertaking proved successful in every respect. The work coming
within the limits of men of small means, a
large list of subscribers in our principal
towns and cities was obtained.

During his eager study of the habits of
birds, Audubon had made very full notes of
the characteristics of the wild animals of our
country, and had prepared some drawings
of them. And now, although he was nearly
seventy years of age, he entered with all
the vigor of his youth upon the work of pre-
paring as faithful a representation of the
quadrupeds as he had of the birds of his native land. With the treasures of his previous
researches and experience, and with a reso-
lution equal to all the difficulties in his path,
he began to arrange his materials, and was
soon deep in the prosecution of the work.
Dr. Bachman, his unfailing and learned friend
of Charleston, and his two sons were united
with him in the enterprise. To enable him
to perfect this work, he projected the journey to the Rocky Mountains; but his family
earnestly and successfully resisted his inten-
tions, not deeming it prudent for one so
far advanced in years to undergo so long
and wearisome a tour. It was well, as the

event proved, that he remained in his quiet and beautiful home, and in the bosom of his affectionate family.

A folio volume, entitled the "Quadrupeds of America," was published in 1850, together with a "Biography of American Quadrupeds." These volumes bear the characteristic marks of his faithfulness and enthusiastic love for the instinctive creatures of God. They also concluded his labors for his race, and completed a monument to his reputation which will remain when the stone over his tomb crumbles to the dust.

While still busily engaged in the collection of materials for succeeding volumes his powers of mind and body began to give way. "The once brilliant eye could no longer keenly inspect the minute organs of the smaller quadrupeds and birds, nor could the once firm hand trace aught but trembling lines. We have heard that the last gleam of light stole across his features a few days before his death, when one of his sons held before him, as he sat in his chair, some of his most cherished drawings." *

He gently "fell on sleep" on the 27th of January, 1851. He rested from his long,

* "Homes of American Authors."

self-sacrificing labors, but "his works do follow him." No life that is consecrated to the well-being or improvement of society and to the glory of God can be lost; it becomes a permanent and active power upon the earth.

THE END.

.